LUCY'S CHANCE

By the Author

Lands End

Lucy's Chance

The After Dark Series:

Infiltration

Pursuit

LUCY'S CHANCE

by
Jackie D

2017

LUCY'S CHANCE

ISBN 13: 978-1-63555-027-6

THIS TRADE PAPERBACK ORIGINAL IS PUBLISHED BY
BOLD STROKES BOOKS, INC.
P.O. BOX 249
VALLEY FALLS, NY 12185

FIRST EDITION: DECEMBER 2017

CREDITS
EDITORS: VICTORIA VILLASENOR AND CINDY CRESAP
PRODUCTION DESIGN: SUSAN RAMUNDO
COVER DESIGN BY MELODY POND

Acknowledgments

Thank you to the Bold Strokes team, for your continued support. Especially, Vic Villasenor and Cindy Cresap for helping fill in all the missing pieces, even when you have had to tell me several times over. Thank you to my mom for always reading and pointing out any and everything that was missed (I promise I will figure out the whole "preposition at the end of a sentence thing" one day). Thank you, Alexis, for always supporting my desire to create these worlds and live in them for a bit. And last but not least, the readers who keep cracking open the books to escape with me for a little while. Your words of encouragement and appreciation mean everything.

Dedication

For my sister, Julie.
You've turned into such an awesome adult.
I continue to be in awe of your courage and bravery,
every day you put on that badge; and your ability
to consume impressive amounts of funny tasting cider.
I'm glad Mom didn't listen when I told her to put you
back on the day you were born. I love you.

CHAPTER ONE

Lucy Rodriguez heard the clicking back and forth along the side of her bed. The small circles were next, and then the whimpering. She pulled herself over to the corner and peeked out from underneath the covers. A golden puff of happiness and fluff danced back and forth with her leash in her mouth.

"No, Holly." She moaned. "Just five more minutes."

The dog paused, blinking. Holly knew just as well as she did that it wouldn't be five more minutes. Lucy would get up now to do her bidding. The Pomeranian had become the boss the day she brought her home from the rescue shelter. The only thing that changed in the last two years was that Holly gained a little more control every day.

"Don't look at me like that."

Holly did another small circle and added a bounce for good measure.

"Fine." She pulled the covers off and swung her feet over the side of the bed. She took a moment to stretch, trying to roll the kinks out of her neck and shoulders, which had been there now as long as she could remember. The small, tight knots were remnants and a constant reminder of the fitful sleep that had become her norm in recent years.

Lucy shuffled over to the chair and pulled on the sweatshirt she had thrown in a heap the night before. She grabbed her cell and keys while putting on her flip-flops. She stared down at Holly who was still bouncing with her leash in her mouth, waiting for their morning trek downstairs.

"After you, Your Majesty." She pulled the door open and allowed Holly to traipse ahead.

The elevator slowly descended the twelve levels of her apartment building. Holly sat facing the doors as if she were awaiting her loyal subjects. The elevator bounced to a stop, and Holly knowingly wagged her tail. She bounded out of the elevator and took a left, heading toward the outdoor pool area.

Once outside, Lucy unhooked Holly from her leash and let her wander. The fluff ball immediately headed over to the small grass area and started her morning ritual of sniffing each square inch. Lucy sat down on one of the lounge chairs and clicked the email icon on the lower portion of her phone screen. There was nothing too earth-shattering—a few coupons from her favorite online shoe store, an Evite for a coworker's thirtieth birthday, and two from her mom. She opened the first.

Lucy,
I haven't heard from you in a week. Is everything okay? I don't know why you have to live in San Diego. There are plenty of newspapers here, near your family.

She opened the next email.

I forgot to say, Love, Mom.
Love, Mom

Lucy laughed. She could set her watch by the repetitiveness of this conversation. Her parents wanted her near them, just like her other three siblings. They never understood why she left Northern California to go to school in San Diego. They understood even less why she took a job overseas as a reporter. Their frustration hit its paramount when she left that job and took one with a newspaper in San Diego when she got back. The answer was simple, and one she'd never share with them. She couldn't live in Clearbrook without seeing Erica, and she couldn't see Erica without wishing she could undo an irrational night twelve years ago, when she foolishly threw away the one and only person who had ever owned her heart, thus changing the course of her life forever.

She flopped backward onto the lounge chair. Holly came trotting over and stuck her nose against her cheek. Realizing Lucy was fine and just being theatrical, she went back to her inspection of the various pieces of purposefully placed furniture around the patio area.

"You'd be a jerk of a human," she said to her.

"Ugh. What are you moping about now?" Grayson took a seat next to her on the lounge chair. He folded his robe over his legs and sipped his coffee. Grayson, with his perfectly manicured nails, shaped eyebrows, and chiseled features, was her best friend and voice of reason.

"My mom wants me to come home."

Holly, being the traitor she always was when Grayson was around, hurried over. She did her best twirl and booty shake, which earned her a nuzzle to the face and a kiss on the nose.

Grayson turned and looked at her, still scratching behind Holly's ears. "So, go home. You always talk about how wonderful Clearbrook is, how you had such an amazing childhood, blah, blah, blah."

Lucy pulled her hood tightly over her head and chewed on the strings. "No."

"Always so dramatic." He tugged on the small opening she had created to breathe. "Just go. Make Mama happy."

"You say that because she likes you better than me."

He leaned back on one arm, his leg swinging up and down. "Your mother has impeccable taste."

"You just finally got her hair to the right color. Now she comes every six weeks, just to see you. I'm a sideshow."

"Like I said, impeccable taste."

"You could come with me. Just for the weekend." She offered her brightest smile, hoping to appeal to his sense of loyalty.

Grayson was not only a perfect buffer but was a retreat she could escape to if things went off the rails.

"Oh, no. I hear they have a five gay limit up there. I don't want to tip the scales and throw off the equilibrium for the rest of us. I wouldn't be able to show my face at Pride ever again."

"I hate you." She pulled the strings again, making the hole around her face barely the size of a silver dollar. She knew the habit annoyed Grayson, but she couldn't help herself. She had pulled on the strings of her sweatshirts since she was a kid, something she didn't really think about until she started seeing a therapist. Her mother always said her facial expressions gave away whatever she was feeling, despite what she said. She tried to be more cognizant of these behaviors, and now she peeped out of her self-created cave to look at Grayson pleadingly.

He stood and grabbed Holly's leash, shooing off her comment with a single, elegant hand movement. "See how much you hate me when you pick up Holly tonight and I've babied her with fresh bacon and massages all day."

"Thanks for watching her."

He blew her a kiss and strolled back inside. Holly never bothered to glance back. *Typical.*

She sat rooted in her spot for a few more moments. The morning sun was starting to radiate its potency, and the pricks of heat felt wonderful on her skin. The thought of going home squelched her moment of enjoyment. She loved her family, and she missed them terribly, but having to see Erica was too painful. Seeing Erica when she was home, or more accurately, *not* seeing Erica, tore at her insides. If she was honest, she wasn't even sure how they'd gotten here. The situation seemed to have spiraled out of her control. At first, she avoided Erica because she knew how badly she had hurt her and couldn't bear to see the pain in her eyes. Then, after a while, the avoidance became a habit, and she worried it had moved past the point of reconnection. She feared the awkwardness of being together, in a situation where talking would tarnish the memories she held so close. All she had left of Erica were those memories, and she couldn't bear to part with them.

❖

Erica Chance watched the last few seconds tick off the timer of her treadmill. It began to slow, and then thankfully turned to a walk. A familiar throb thrummed from her right ankle, and she tried to shake it out as she continued her pace.

"I'm getting old, Bella."

The basset hound continued to lie on the couch and shifted her head slightly at her name. Her oversized paws remained crossed in front of her as she lay on her side. One of her ears flopped over her mouth, covering her nose.

Erica hopped off the machine and headed toward the bathroom. Her morning routine of breakfast, followed by a run on the treadmill, was as close as she came to going to church. She reveled in the consistency and dependability of routine in general. Her cell phone rang, redirecting her to the kitchen counter. At first, she thought she hadn't heard the dispatcher correctly, but upon asking for a repeat, she knew what she was saying was true. There was a body at the old Miller Farm, and she needed to report there immediately.

Erica had been with the Clearbrook Police Department for ten years, and there had never been a murder. There had been robberies, theft, and even a few domestic violence cases, but never a murder.

She hung up the phone and for a moment, wasn't sure what to do next. She leaned against the counter, feeling a bit sick to her stomach. If there was a murder, the likelihood of knowing the victim was high in this community. She stared at Bella, wishing she could talk to her. Of course, even if she could, that would mean catching her in a moment she was actually awake and lucid. Bella was thoroughly engaged in a level of sleep Erica would never be able to achieve. Over the years, Erica had become accustomed to nights of fitful rest. Images of abused women, abandoned children, and drunk-driving accidents haunted her dreams. These instances managed to weave their way through her slumbering thoughts. She couldn't remember a morning where she woke up feeling completely rested.

She texted her partner, Diego Rodriguez, to let him know she would pick him up as soon as she showered. On her way to the bathroom, she patted Bella on the head. This unexpected jostle was enough to wake the lump, but just barely. Erica could hear the snores before she opened the shower door. Bella had become a source of therapy over the years. Regardless of how chaotic her day had been, no matter how uneventful her love life was at the time, Bella was consistent. She knew what to expect, and that was not only comforting, it was needed.

Thirty minutes later, she pulled up outside Diego's house. He was already waiting outside, ready for the day. But today wouldn't be like any other day they had ever spent together. He got in the car, but he didn't greet her with his usual smile. Instead, he was somber. He shared her worry, and the concern shadowed his face and darkened his eyes. Usually, they would stop at the local bagel shop, get coffee, and head to the station. Any other day, they would spend this time in the car talking about his children and his wife. They would talk about Bella and what their plans were for the weekend. But this morning, neither of them said anything as Erica maneuvered down the familiar streets, heading for the back roads of their native town.

Erica had known Diego and the rest of his family for as long as she could remember. There wasn't a single significant milestone in her life where the Rodriguez family hadn't been there. Everything from first home runs to first heartbreaks, the family couldn't have been more a part of her if they had shared a bloodline. Everyone from the matriarch of the family, Grandma Rodriguez, to the newest member, Sofia, held a special place in her heart. But none more so than his sister, Lucy. Lucy had left a fracture in her soul she still felt to this day.

They pulled up to the old farm and drove past the broken, rusted gate. Erica took the car down the dry, mocha colored dirt road. Dust and rocks popped from behind the tires, leaving a sandy cloud in their wake. The scene was easy to see. Even from five hundred feet away, there was no mistaking something significant had taken place. Five police cruisers, all the department owned, were parked with their lights still flashing.

The last time Erica had stepped foot on the Miller property was during high school. Sam Miller had thrown a party while his parents were out of town for the weekend, and everyone in their junior class had attended, or that's how it had seemed anyway. She remembered walking to her car along this dirt road, in the midst of her classmates in various stages of drunken exploration. It had been a great party that was talked about for weeks after. Now, these flashing lights would be the memory she flipped to whenever someone mentioned the Miller property. The night of teenage fun and excitement would fade away, leaving a life cut short in its place. Erica took a deep breath as they got out of the car. It would've been a beautiful spring morning. The dampness of the morning dew was still thick in the air, cooling everything it wrapped itself around. She came around the side of the car, mentally bracing herself for what she was about to see. The uniformed police officers parted, letting Erica and Diego through.

"What do we know?" Erica asked.

Jake Newton, the newest officer on the police force, spoke first. "We got a call from Kenny Miller at around six this morning. He had come up here to take inventory of the farm equipment that's going to auction. He found her here, just like this."

Erica pulled gloves out of her pocket and slid them over her hands. She knelt next to the body, wanting to get a good look at the woman. Erica forced herself to look beyond the mask of blood and dirt. She realized the woman was young, probably somewhere between nineteen to twenty-one. She wore a UC San Diego sweatshirt, blood partially concealing the letters. Her dark brown hair couldn't cover the gaping hole in her head, making it painfully clear she had been hit with a significant amount of force. Erica delicately picked up her hand to look at her fingernails. Under the pink chipped paint, the flesh had been scrubbed clean. Erica stood and took a step back, wanting to take in the whole scene. She had seen her share of upsetting scenes since becoming a police officer, but nothing like this. She had seen dead bodies at the scenes of car accidents, had witnessed bleeding women and children at the hands of an angry spouse. She had investigated a few suicides over the years. Over time, she had learned to divorce herself from the feelings of the victims to do her job. But this was different, not because of her age, or her injuries, although those were disturbing enough. No, this was different because it was her first murder, a sign that her quiet town of Clearbrook wasn't safe from the violence of the bigger cities. She tried to force down the fear and concentrate.

Diego, who had been silent, turned toward the other officers. "We need everyone to back up." He motioned with his hands. "Tape off the entire farm. No one in or out except authorized personnel. Take Kenny down to the station and get the coroner out here."

He pulled a camera out of his bag and started taking pictures. Erica watched him carefully, trying to gauge his frame of mind. She needed the reassurance that his feelings echoed her own and she wasn't reacting like some first-day rookie. Diego was normally happy, full of energy. But right now, his brown skin was pale and clammy. His lips had lost a bit of their color, and his eyes were rimmed red. He moved around the scene, snapping picture after picture.

Erica chewed on her bottom lip, frustrated that her department wasn't adequately equipped to deal with this type of scene. There were footprints all around the body. Most were probably from the officers, but a few could've been from the psycho who had dumped the poor woman here, a lonely and barren final resting place. She scanned the woman's clothes and the area surrounding her, but there were no distinct dust or drag marks. *He carried her to this location.* Which also meant this wasn't the murder site. Erica felt the woman's pockets, looking for a wallet or anything that could help them identify her.

"Her name is Claudia Ramos," Diego said from behind her.

Erica stood and looked at him. Diego was struggling to hold it together, just like her, but for different reasons. She had been relieved when she didn't recognize the victim right away, but it hadn't occurred to her the same wasn't true for Diego.

Diego took another picture. "Her father works as a groundskeeper at the high school."

Erica's breath caught in her chest. She put a hand on his shoulder, and he took another picture.

"She graduated three years ago. She's pre-med at UC San Diego, full academic scholarship. She was home visiting for spring break. My wife and I ran into her and her father at the store last Saturday."

"I'm sorry." Those two words weren't good enough, not by a long shot, but she wasn't sure what else to say. Diego had always been stable, rational, and focused. He was rarely off-kilter, and because of that, she wasn't sure how to ease his pain.

"Let's just make sure we do everything right so we can catch this guy." His eyes were filled with tears now. He put the camera back over his face and moved to the left, continuing to take pictures.

"Agreed."

"And, Chance, I want to be the one who notifies the family."

"Okay, let's finish up here and then we'll head over."

Erica knew that notifying the family would be no easy task. Even when it was an accident, the loss of a loved one was a raw and emotional experience. This notification wouldn't be like the others because they had no explanation, no leads, nothing. And even if they were able to walk into this family's home and tell them they had all the information they needed, it wouldn't be good enough, not when their daughter had been savagely murdered and dumped. To make matters worse, Diego knew these people, and their burden would become his own. Watching her partner, her friend, go through the pain of having to break the news to this family would be heartbreaking. She wished she could shield him from that pain; she wished she could shield them all. However, those weren't the options in front of her now. All she could do was be there for him and find the bastard that did this.

Erica had always loved the idea of being a police officer. She had naively believed that the world fell into nice, neat little categories. You could place any person into the good category or the bad. The justice system would handle the people who fell into the bad category and take care of everyone else. She had believed that if she did her job correctly, she would help keep bad things from happening to good people. But like most things in life, it wasn't that simple.

She had never considered how the evil would continue to seep into the good people, long after the immediate threat had been removed. The long-term damage done by an abusive parent clung to the affected child like a wet shirt. The victims of drunk-driving accidents didn't stop at the accident. The suffering would trickle through the community, claiming victims emotionally.

Of course, along with the bad, there were always glimmers of good. The troubled teenager she helped redirect after he was caught shoplifting from the grocery store. The several summers she had spent coaching kids in the Police Activities League. She had even spent two hours every Saturday her first two years on the force being called out to the Snyder property, just to check for intruders. As it turned out, Mrs. Snyder was just incredibly lonely and would call in because she wanted someone to chat with for a bit. Erica went every time, not because she believed an intruder would be there but because she thought it was the right thing to do for the elderly woman. If she needed someone to talk to that badly, Erica had no problem being that person.

These moments of aid and community service were what Erica clung to, and she used them as a shield from the others. The others burrowed their way into her mind, changing not only her sleep patterns but the way she saw the world. Those moments were the broadcasters of the realization that you couldn't save them all.

The best you could do was to give the victims the first piece of the puzzle to help them start reassembling their lives. It wouldn't be the life they had grown up wanting, it wouldn't be what they pictured for themselves or their loved ones, but it would be a beginning. Erica, Diego, and everyone who wore a badge were the guardians of these pieces. The ones entrusted to retrieve them and return them to their rightful owners. She took a deep breath and squared her shoulders, forcing herself to focus. The young woman on the ground deserved nothing but her best.

Chapter Two

Lucy sat in the bullpen, listening to her colleagues pitch ideas to their editor. Each of them was tossing out concepts with the intention of impressing their boss. There were two ways a story ended up in a newspaper. The first was a tip from the public. An editor received an unfathomable amount of calls and emails from the public on any given day. They sorted through those reports and weeded out the stories that needed to be followed up on, separating those events from the rest. Lucy had decided long ago she would never want that responsibility for any salary. In general, the public was a fickle and demanding group. Their interests and willingness to make almost any event into headline news wasn't something she wanted on her shoulders. The second way a story came to fruition was because a reporter had found a lead into something of interest. They pitched the ideas to the editor and got the go-ahead. Choosing a story to follow was what Lucy preferred. She liked having the ability to go in the direction she saw fit, and it was a privilege she had earned in her years with this paper and before, from her time in the field. She had earned her stripes, so to say.

One of the interns rushed in, carrying a cup of coffee balanced on top of a stack of files. A chair backed into him, causing the coffee to spill all over the floor and the editor. The intern ducked behind the chair, presumably to clean up the spill. Lucy thought back to a day she had also been cleaning up a spill.

"Don't worry about it." Erica stood over her as Lucy tried to sop up the splattered soda with a rag she had found on the garage workbench.

"Your grandpa's going to be so mad at us. He keeps this place perfect."

Erica knelt next to her. She put her hand on top of hers to stop her movements. "He'll just say not to cry over spilled milk."

Lucy had a response ready because she knew exactly what Erica was going to say. But now, she couldn't force her mouth to form the words. Not with Erica's hand on top of her own. Her hand tingled in a way it never had before. It felt like someone had lightly kissed her where it rested. It hadn't done that when Troy had held her hand, and she hadn't felt the rush of warmth she felt now when Shaun had kissed her, either.

She pulled her hand back, worried it would transfer to Erica somehow and she would know what she was feeling. When she finally met Erica's crystal blue eyes, she saw it. Erica had felt it too, the simplest of connections, the softest of touches, that somehow changed everything. Lucy didn't know what it meant. She couldn't find the words to describe the warm sensation bubbling up in her belly, making her want to giggle. She moved closer to Erica not knowing anything except that she wanted, needed, to be near her.

Erica stood, shoving her hands in her pockets, swaying back and forth, staring at the ground. Her shaggy blond hair fell in her face, momentarily blocking her eyes. "Want to go watch TRL?"

"Lucy."

Lucy heard her name and pulled herself back into the moment. She looked around the room, unsure who had been trying to get her attention. Blank looks coming from several faces around the table met her gaze.

"Where are you on the Shrine trial?"

Oh, that's right, this is my life. "It'll be on your desk by five."

Her editor nodded and moved on unceremoniously. In her early days, Lucy had covered international affairs, the war in the Middle East, and other military areas. Now she was on the crime beat, and lucky for her, there was never a shortage of material in San Diego.

Lucy looked outside. Clouds moved at a leisurely pace across the pale blue sky. It would be a perfect day to go to the beach. It wouldn't be painfully crowded yet, the way San Diego beaches often were when the weather started to heat up. There was still a chill in the air, left over from the changing seasons. By this afternoon, the temperature would be tipping close to the mid-seventies. She could take off the rest of the day, call Grayson, and have him and Holly meet her down at Mission Beach. When was the last time she blew off work? *Never. Obviously.*

Those thoughts were interrupted by her editor's voice once again. "Rodriguez?"

Jesus, pay attention. "Yeah, boss?"

"Want to take the lead on the Syrian refugee crisis?"

No, she did not want to take the lead on the Syrian refugee crisis. She had been very explicit when she came to work for this paper that she would no longer be covering international affairs. She had spent seven years in the bowels of the war in the Middle East, and she had no intention of going back, physically or emotionally. Luckily for her, there were reporters sitting around her who had career ambitions that eclipsed her own on the subject. She shook her head.

A recent college grad immediately raised his hand. "I'll take it."

Her editor slid the file across the table, and he enthusiastically grabbed it and started flipping through the papers. She remembered when she was like that, fearless with a touch of optimism that hadn't been squelched by the problems of the real world. She almost envied his naivety. But that was the age-old tale of irony, not realizing in the moment your vulnerability or your fragile nature. *You just charge in thinking nothing can touch you.* That is, until the day something does, changing your life, and every decision you make after will always be in the shadow of that moment.

Lucy had already experienced three destiny markers that had changed her life forever and often thought how frustrating it was not knowing their significance at the time. Sure, one was obvious, but the others, she hadn't felt the effect of until long after they had passed. The first was when she had discovered journalism in her freshman year of college. She hadn't known it was her calling until she'd felt the rush of her first story being published in her college's newspaper. In that one instant she'd been hooked, and she never looked back. She had immediately changed her major from business to journalism. Seeing her name in headlines still gave her the same rush she had felt the first time.

Another was the day she couldn't bear to go back to the war-ravaged Middle East. The decision hadn't been premeditated, and in fact, she didn't realize she had made it until she had arrived at the airport. Lucy felt her heart rate pick up at the memory of that day. She practiced the breathing techniques she had learned in therapy, pushing the thoughts back down and out of her current train of thought. She had gotten better at it over the years, and now she could go weeks, sometimes months, without having to invoke the practice.

"Rodriguez, you're from Clearbrook, right?" her editor asked.

"Clearbrook, California?"

He looked confused. She wasn't on her game today, and he knew it. "Yeah, up near San Francisco."

"Yeah, why?"

"A UC San Diego student was killed up there two days ago. Find out what's going on."

Someone was killed in Clearbrook? What the hell? "You got it, boss."

Her editor stood, signaling the end of their meeting. Everyone else in the room followed suit, filing out the doors and heading to their assigned tasks.

Lucy hurried to her desk and pulled up the website for the local newspaper. Nothing was there, but that made sense. It only released a weekly periodical. If it happened two days ago, nothing would be in print yet. She checked social media accounts for UC San Diego and found the "In Memoriam" messages from student after student, detailing their remorse. Claudia Ramos seemed to have the world at her fingertips, and by all accounts she was bright, funny, and beautiful. *What a waste.*

Lucy scrolled through the messages until she found one where the person had changed their profile picture to one of her and the victim in a friendly embrace. Lucy wanted to talk to someone who knew the victim personally. She sent a message requesting a phone call.

While she waited for a response, she pulled up the website for Clearbrook High School and looked through their online yearbooks. It only took a few searches to find Claudia. The things people were saying weren't exaggerated by any means. She was salutatorian of her class, class treasurer, she took part in yearbook, leadership, and played two varsity sports. She printed the information out and continued looking.

Lucy let the mouse hover over another archive, her graduating class from thirteen years ago. She didn't need to open the file because she knew what was in those pages. Those old photos and somewhat recognizable names were nothing but a reminder of what and who she had given up. What she had given up was her third destiny marker. The choice she had made that night had impacted every single day since then and would continue to for the remainder of her life. Lucy couldn't deal with that right now, and her nerves wouldn't allow it. She closed the page and checked to see if the young woman had responded. Surprisingly, there was already a message along with a phone number.

CHAPTER THREE

He sat on the couch to admire his work. This one had been much easier than the last. No scratching or screaming. All it had taken was sleight of hand, a quick slip of a bit of extra liquid into a drink. Now she was his and his alone. The knowledge was invigorating, intoxicating, and addicting. Now was the hard part. He had to wait for her to wake up. He hated waiting, hated having to temper his excitement while the drug worked through their systems. But what else was he supposed to do? She needed to be awake to enjoy it, and he wasn't a monster; he wouldn't touch her without her knowledge. No, that's not what he was about at all.

He had known he wanted her from the first time he saw her. It was like the planets had aligned, bringing her in for a simple salad and a diet soda just when he was there to appreciate all she was. Luckily, she had been the only patron that day, and by the time she stumbled outside to get in her car, feeling sick, it wasn't much work to grab her. After all, she was destined to be with him, so he was just taking what was already his.

Her eyes fluttered, indicating she was waking up. He watched the terror eclipse her face as she started to realize what had happened. She tried moving her arms and hands, but it wouldn't do her any good. Zip ties and duct tape were essential tools in his bag; he had learned his lesson. Her eyes bulged when she tried to scream against the tape, and the fear he saw warmed his chest.

He walked over and put his hand on her head. "Shh. It's okay, no one can hear you, and you'll want to save your strength."

She moved to get away from his hand, trying to pull her body along the dirt floor. The attempt would be futile, but it didn't matter. He wanted her to have hope, a will to live. The longer she was willing to fight, the longer he could keep her. And he wanted to keep her.

"Let me know I can trust you and I'll give you some water. How long that takes is up to you."

The girl continued to try to scream as she dragged her legs across the dirt floor. She didn't understand there was nowhere to go, but she would. This was one of his favorite aspects of Rohypnol, or as it was known on the streets, a roofie. It rendered its victim paralyzed, and even when they started to come to, it was hard to control the muscles and the mind. It had the strength of ten Valium and was ridiculously easy to get. He would pre-mix it with a bit of water, dissolving the contents, and then pour it into whoever's drink he determined worthy. Sure, it was difficult for her to move around now, but it was for her own good. If she had complete control of her faculties, she would try to fight back, possibly escape, and that wouldn't end well for her. No, this was for her own good, protection from herself.

"I'm going to give you some time to think about it." He touched her again and leaned down to kiss the top of her head, now that she had finally halted her movements toward the staircase. She bucked, knocking him in the lip, leaving a twinge of copper in his mouth. He pressed his fists into his side, fighting the urge to smack her across the face. He tamped down his anger, wanting her to realize the depths of his kindness. She would realize soon enough that her life was a gift he was bestowing on her, simply out of his desire to have her in his world. That ability to keep the desire alive rested purely on her willingness to be a grateful and willing participant.

He walked up the staircase to a metal door. "That's your one freebie." He turned off the light and locked the door behind him. She would come around, there was no doubt in his mind. And if she didn't, he would just find a new one and start over. The result would be her fault, not his. She was the one making things difficult on herself.

CHAPTER FOUR

Erica hung up the phone and walked back over to the large table they'd been working from for the last three days. She lifted her coffee cup and realized it was empty again. She'd lost track of how many times she'd filled it up in the last seventy-two hours. *One more isn't going to hurt.* Diego seemed to have read her mind, and a moment later he was pouring the dark, burnt liquid into her mug.

"Thanks."

"Okay, so we have the timeline pretty much nailed down at this point. She met up with some friends for lunch at Vicki's Sandwich Shop, at around twelve thirty. After that, she stopped by Clearbrook High to see one of her old teachers, Mrs. Redding, and talked to her for approximately forty-five minutes. Then, she goes home for the afternoon. She hangs out with her little brother, watches television, and gets on social media. She told her parents she had plans to go out with some friends to see a movie that night. She leaves to go on a run at four o'clock, stops by Starbucks to get a green tea, and is never heard from again."

"The cell company says she made two phone calls before going for her run. The first was to one of her girlfriends she had plans to go have drinks with at Junior's, and the other was to her roommate down in San Diego. We were able to track her run through the GPS on her phone, but it goes completely dead right outside of Starbucks."

"Her parents said they weren't aware of any boyfriend. We need to follow up on that."

"I spoke with her roommate, and she says Claudia wasn't seeing anyone."

"It doesn't make any sense. It's like she just disappeared. How could no one see someone take her?"

"I know."

Diego looked at her, and the fatigue setting in around his eyes made him look older than his thirty-five years. Neither of them had ever worked a case of this magnitude, and knowing the victim was making his burden even greater. She knew it would be like this until they solved the case and probably for some time after. "Why don't you go home and have dinner with your wife and kids?"

"Is that who called you?"

"She said you weren't answering your cell." Erica shrugged.

"I can't just go home and have dinner. Not while he's still out there."

She leaned across the table and flipped the file shut. "It will be good to walk away, take a break. Come back tomorrow with fresh eyes. We haven't left the station in three days. Your family needs you too."

She could tell he was about to protest and then changed his mind. "Okay, Chance. Maybe you're right. I'd love to sleep in my bed and not on one of these lumpy couches."

He grabbed his suit jacket off the back of the chair and threw it over his arm. "You're going home too, right?"

"Yeah, just have to stop and see Sheila first, then pick up Bella."

"Uh-oh."

"What, uh-oh?"

"I know that look. You're breaking up with Sheila, aren't you?"

"How did you get that out of what I said? And besides, you can't break up with someone you aren't really dating. We hang out, sure, but there's nothing official."

"It's not what you said, but how you said it. I've known you damn near your whole life, and I know when you're done with someone. Besides, you're at your four-month mark, and those are the rules."

She crossed her arms, frustrated with him for knowing her so well, and with herself for being so predictable. "It's not a rule."

For the first time in three days, he laughed. "It might as well be. I've never seen someone last longer than four months."

They both knew that wasn't true, but they had an unspoken agreement not to talk about her relationship with Lucy. "If you don't know if they're the one in—"

"In four months, then they're not the one," he finished for her. "Yeah, yeah, I've heard it before."

"It's a good rule," she murmured. She could attempt to explain the rule to Diego again, but what was the point? A rule like this was born from pure heartbreak, and Diego had never experienced anything like that. He never had to question whether or not his soul was still intact simply because someone was no longer in his life. He had never experienced the need to push your car over the hundred miles per hour barrier just to feel something other than anguish. He had never awoken at night to find the pillow you're clutching wet with tears because even your subconscious mind knows a part of you is missing. No, Diego would never understand. She would allow his questions to remain unanswered because there were no words to do those feelings justice.

Holly dragged the fourth toy to the middle of the room and made a whimpering sound.

"She wants you to play with her."

"I know, Grayson, but I'm trying to finish this last bit of research."

He sat on the couch and Holly jumped on his lap, toys forgotten. "Maybe you wouldn't have to do so much digging if you just, say, went home. And don't tell me you're already there. You know what I mean." He took a sip from his wine glass.

"Snarkiness noted." She glanced over, pulled the glass from his hand, and took a giant gulp.

"Heathen." He took the glass back.

"I can't just go back and do the story."

"Didn't you say your brother is assigned to the case?" He ran his finger around the lip of the glass.

"Yes, that's what my mom said."

"Don't you get along with him?"

"Yeah, I get along great with both my brothers." She crossed her arms.

"Okay, you're seriously going to have to fill me in because I'm apparently missing something."

She pulled the wine glass out of his hand again and took another gulp. He smacked her hand as she gave it back. "I poured you your own, and it's right next to you." He pointed to the table.

"Oh, thanks." She picked the glass up and took another gulp. "His partner won't want to see me, and I do my best not to upset her...anymore." She spun the stem of the wineglass between her two fingers, trying to picture Erica's reaction to seeing her again. She wasn't sure what it would be, and not knowing was painful.

Grayson looked at her blankly for a moment and then squeezed her arm with the excitement of a small child. "Oh my God, please tell me his partner is Erica, *the* Erica."

She finished off what was in her glass and set it back on the table. "The one and only." She pulled his tightly gripped fingers from her arm.

"Oh, that's perfect. Honey, this is your chance."

"She's not *my* chance. Not anymore."

He blinked at her, annoyance flickering in his eyes. "Even you saying that tells me you want her to be. But it's your chance to win her back. Jesus, how many hours have I spent listening to you blather on and on about this woman? Now you have a real reason to be there with her, to talk to her, and I'm not going to let you miss it."

She scratched Holly behind the ears. "Believe me when I tell you, Erica Chance wants nothing to do with me."

"Sweet baby Jesus, her last name is Chance?" He clapped. "Oh, I love it."

"I thought you just said you listened to me blather on and on about her, but you didn't even know her last name."

"I assumed you were being ironic. Plus, I kind of tune you out when you get like that."

"I don't even know why we're friends."

He got off the couch, grabbed her wine glass, and walked into the kitchen. "Because I cut your hair perfectly, watch the precious angel, and because I'm going to go with you to Clearbrook."

She swung around on the couch. "I thought you didn't want to tip the proverbial gay scale, or whatever you called it."

He shook his finger back and forth. "I'm not going to let you mess this up, scale be damned."

"If I go, I'm going there to work."

He was practically skipping back toward the couch. "It's like a mission. Can I give it a code name?"

"No."

"I'm going to give it a code name."

"You aren't coming."

"Mission Lezbos."

"No."

"Mission Pink Taco."

"I hate you."

"Mission Lez-unite."

"I'm never talking to you again."

"Oh, that's the one." He hurried toward the door. "I'm going to go pack!"

She turned and looked at Holly. "He took my wine glass." Holly's tail wagged back and forth. "Traitor."

She *should* go to Clearbrook to write this story, because in any other situation she would be packing her bags. Seeing a place, feeling the scene and surroundings, and actually talking to the people involved always made for a better story than Google Maps and phone calls. Plus, maybe things would be different now. It had been years since she had been face-to-face with Erica, so maybe she would want to see her. They had been everything to each other at one point, best friends, lovers, partners. Surely, Erica knew that what they had was real. If there was even a part of Erica that missed her, just a sliver of feelings that remained of what they once shared, shouldn't she take the chance?

Chapter Five

He watched her labored movements with anticipation. She could barely hold herself up, and the exhaustion, dehydration, and hunger were setting in. He could see it in her eyes. He ran his hand along the side of her face, and for the first time, she didn't flinch. "I'm going to pull the tape off now. But if you make a sound, any sound, that will be it."

She nodded her understanding, and he pulled the tape off. He unscrewed the cap from the water bottle, and her eyes were fixated on his movements. She was exactly where he wanted her to be now, dependent on him. He held the bottle up to her mouth and tipped it up, letting the water flow past her lips. She drank it down greedily, gulping and pulling with her mouth, causing the sides of the plastic to cave in. When it was gone, he tossed it to the side, keeping his gaze focused on her, waiting to see the hope return.

"Please, I'm still thirsty." Her voice was cracked.

"You get one bottle a day."

"Why?"

He could feel the anger rising from his belly, but he tried to push it back down. "Because those are the rules."

"The rules of what?" She coughed.

"The rules of our arrangement."

His response apparently angered her. She squinted at him, and her face flushed red. "People will be looking for me. You can't possibly think you'll get away with this."

Why did she have to say that? Why couldn't she just be grateful for what he was doing? Why did she need to test him? "I saved you."

She shifted her weight from kneeling to legs out in front. This actually made him more comfortable. The position left her more vulnerable, less agile. She didn't realize her unconscious change in weight distribution was a sign of resignation. Another step closer to conformity.

"You saved me? What the hell did you save me from?"

He went to his makeshift workbench and moved items around. "I saved you from yourself. You should have more respect."

"Respect? Respect for what?"

He let his fingers slide over the top of the hammer, feeling them twitch at the draw to pick it up. "For me! The only reason you're still breathing is because I've decided to let you."

Her face paled at his words. "I want to go home. I won't tell anyone. Please just let me go."

He had heard it before, with the same cadence and tone. They were all the same, so very disappointing. "You aren't going anywhere." Next would come the pleading, the tears, and then the bargaining would complete the speech he knew so well.

"Please, I'll give you whatever you want, just please let me go. My parents have money. Do you want money?"

"Money? No, I don't want any money. I want you to understand your actions have consequences. I want you to realize what you've done."

Her expression was more desperate now, bordering on pathetic. "I honestly have no idea what you're talking about."

"You're a tease."

He watched her eyes as fear transitioned to realization, her behavior finally coming into focus. "Oh my God, I remember you now."

He ripped off a piece of duct tape, and before she could go on, he covered her mouth again. He didn't want to hear any of her excuses. It was too late for that.

CHAPTER SIX

"Did you even go home last night?" Diego said as he took his seat opposite Erica on their adjoined desks.

"Yes, I went home. I have a dog, you know."

"Bella is more of a loveable lump than a dog."

"Careful, she'll know what you said."

"No doubt, with those ridiculous ears of hers."

Diego was in a better mood today, laughing and joking around. It was a nice reprieve from staring down the biggest case either of them had ever seen. "How's the family?"

He sipped his coffee. "Good. We expect to see you tomorrow night for dinner."

"I'll be there."

"You can bring Sheila."

Erica pushed the pencil on her desk back and forth. "Okay, I'll see if she's busy."

"See if she's busy? It's your birthday. What else would she be doing?"

She started spinning the pencil now. "I don't know, I'm sure she's got stuff to do. I don't expect her life to revolve around me."

"Chance, it's your birthday for Christ's sake. Is she still your girlfriend, or what?"

"You know I hate labels."

"Uh-huh. Hate labels like *girlfriend*. I thought you saw her last night? So, it wasn't a date?"

"I'm bringing Bella for sure. You can put me down for a plus one on that count. And Sheila and I hang out. Don't make it out to be more than what it is. Last night all I did was stop by to pick up Bella. I asked her to take her for a bit because we had to work late."

"Bella is more of a plus two, the way she eats." He winked at her and started typing, undoubtedly going through the same emails she just had. She also noticed his sidestep of any further discussion of Sheila, which she appreciated.

"Funny."

Her phone rang, and she picked it up while sliding the local paper across the desk toward him. A picture of Claudia Ramos donned the cover, along with pictures of both her and Diego at the scene. The local paper hadn't had much to go on regarding the case, but it was a beautiful tribute to the young woman the town had lost. "Hey, Sheila. What's up?" She purposely didn't turn away from Diego when she saw the name on the caller ID, wanting to prove she had meant what she had said just moments before.

The familiar voice was panicked, random pieces of information spilling from the receiver. "Erica, I'm sorry, you might not even be the person I'm supposed to call. But who do you call for situations like this, the police right? She's missing, and she hasn't been home for two days, which is totally unlike her. My aunt and uncle are freaking out, and with good reason, and no one knows what to do, or who to call."

Erica put the phone on her desk and pushed the speaker button as she motioned for Diego to pay attention. "Sheila, I need you to slow down and tell me exactly what you're talking about."

Diego came around and sat on the corner of her desk, notepad in hand.

"Right, sorry. My cousin, Jessica Vargas, is missing. My aunt and uncle said she was supposed to be home a few days ago. They figured she got hung up at school, and they've been trying to call her cell phone, but it just goes straight to voice mail. We called her boyfriend, and he said she left Sacramento two days ago to come home for the weekend. But no one has seen her, and I'm not sure what to do."

Erica made every effort to keep her voice calm, not wanting to incite any more panic. There were dozens of reasons a college-aged woman might not be home. Reasons which had nothing to do with being legitimately missing, or worse, taken by a man they had yet to identify. She wanted Sheila to hear that reassurance in her voice, but maybe she needed it as well. "Okay, I need you to bring your aunt and uncle down to the station to talk to Diego and me. Can you do that?"

Sheila took a deep breath. "Yes, I can do that. I'll bring them down right away." She paused. "I knew I could count on you. Thanks, babe."

"Sure. See you soon." Erica ended the call and looked at Diego, who was pinching the bridge of his nose.

"Could be nothing," Diego said. The look on his face didn't mirror his words.

She stared at the board, a picture of Claudia Ramos staring back. "Or it could be the beginning."

❖

"The Five is a mess this time of day, we should go around." Lucy put on her blinker and changed lanes. She hit the button on the door, rolling the window up. As it closed, she felt a small tug on her hair. Realizing she had caught a chunk in the window, she quickly cracked the window to set herself free. She glanced over at Grayson to see if he noticed. He smiled and shook his head, no doubt used to her small mishaps by now. Luckily, he didn't dwell on it, continuing the conversation as if nothing happened.

"Honey, we live in California. Every highway is a mess no matter the time of day."

Grayson wasn't wrong, but it didn't mean she wouldn't try to shave off a couple of minutes from their drive. She had somehow temporarily convinced herself this whole thing was a good idea. In a moment of longing to see Erica, she'd made the phone call to her editor saying she'd be willing to head north to check out the story. He happily agreed, leaving her no way to back out if she changed her mind. Now, as she drove down the long open stretch of highway that separated Northern California from Southern California, she felt excitement and apprehension in equal measures. She wasn't sure how Erica would react to her presence, but she needed to know either way. And she couldn't wait to see her family.

"What did your boss say about you coming up here?"

"He was all for it. They don't have to pay for a hotel, and the story is getting covered. It's a win-win."

"I assume you didn't tell them about the secondary mission?"

"There is no secondary mission."

He leaned behind the seat and scratched Holly's ear, who was in her dog seat, buckled in. "That's what she thinks."

"You're impossible."

He pulled out a bag of chips and started munching. "Tell me more about Erica Chance."

"That's not why we're going to Clearbrook."

He rolled his eyes. "Would you humor me, please? We have several hours to kill, and this is how I'd like to spend them."

"What would you like to know?"

"Do you miss the sex?"

"Okay, no more questions." She and Grayson had discussed several of their sexual escapades in the past, but she kept the memories of her time with Erica tucked away in a small corner in her mind. They were her little treasures, tokens for transport to another time where she felt whole.

"Okay, okay, I'll start out a bit softer. How did you two meet?"

"How did we meet? I don't know, I've known her since I was nine. So, I guess at school." She remembered exactly when and how she met Erica, but she also enjoyed aggravating Grayson as often as possible. They'd been in the same class and were assigned seats next to each other. Lucy had forgotten to put her pencil box in her backpack one day and ended up having nothing to write with.

Erica had opened her box and said they could share. They quickly started doing everything together, from tetherball at recess, to walking to and from school.

"Meh, boring. When did you start dating?"

Her first inclination was not to answer any of his questions, but she could feel herself smiling at the memory. "When we were sixteen."

"Are you going to make me ask a thousand questions to get the story out of you in pieces? Could we just skip that?"

She pulled her water bottle out of the console and took a sip. She might have been biding her time with the question, but the water was also a symbol of how she and Erica had started. "I'd dated boys up until Erica. Not tons but enough to know something was always missing. I had fun with them, and I knew they were attractive, but I was never really attracted to them. Does that make sense?"

"Well, not to me, but I understand what you're saying."

"Anyway, Erica and I were laying out by my mom's pool, the summer before our junior year. It was an insanely hot day, something like one hundred and five degrees."

"Holy hell. I hope it's not going to be that hot while we're there."

"Do you want to hear the rest of the story or not?"

He motioned across his lips, zipping them shut.

"I was lying there, not realizing I was staring at her. I wasn't intentionally doing it, but she was just so beautiful. She caught me looking at her, but she didn't tease me or ask what I was doing, she just smiled at me. I knew then I wanted her differently than I had any of the boys I'd dated. I wanted her to touch me, I wanted her to kiss me, I wanted her. The thought had crossed my mind before, but for whatever reason, this time it was more than a passing curiosity, it was a need. I asked her to hand me one of the water bottles out of the cooler, and when she did, I kept hold of her hand. I took a sip out of the bottle, and looking back, I realize I was trying to buy myself time. I guess I wanted to give her a chance to pull away, you know? I put the bottle down and kissed her. I'd never felt anything like it. It was like everything I'd felt like I was missing was suddenly right in front of me. I felt it in every nerve of my body, and I wanted more."

"So, then what happened?"

"We still spent all our time together, but obviously it felt different. We went to movies, ate at each other's houses, did all of the same things, but now we held hands when no one was looking. We made out in every empty room we could find, and believe me, we tried to find as many empty rooms as possible."

He smiled at her. "You get all glowy when you talk about her."

She knew he was right, and she could feel her skin flush at the memory. "She was my first love." The words felt thick as they left her mouth. The weight of their truth was heavy with regret and longing. It made her uncomfortable to say them out loud because the outcome had been so final and all by her own doing. It was embarrassing to admit. She hadn't realized it thirteen years ago, but she knew it now. The finality of such rash decisions leave their mark, a brand burned into the soul and mind. Time might help to heal, but the scars will always remain.

"Has there been a second?"

"No. No, it's always been her. It was her even before we were sixteen, I just didn't realize it yet. I mean, sure, there have been other women. Celibacy has never been a defining attribute of my personality. But no one like Erica. I never felt anything the way I experienced it with her. I never thought of forever, never wanted one. I was stupid enough to think those feelings were common, easy to replicate."

He crunched on a few chips. "How in the world did you manage to fuck that up?"

"Because I'm an idiot." She didn't want to revisit that memory, and she was glad when he seemed to sense that.

"True, but you're my favorite idiot."

"Gee, thanks."

"It's her loss, by the way." He wiped his hands on his pants and took a sip of his soda. "If she doesn't take you back, it would be her loss."

Lucy appreciated that Grayson was trying to be a good friend. But he didn't know Erica. He didn't know how Lucy had treated her and how she had broken her heart. She didn't want to tell him, and more so, she didn't want to say it aloud. It was too painful, too many tears, and too many missed years. Besides, last she heard, Erica had moved on. She was someone else's Chance now. She needed to move on. She needed to look Erica in the eye and know it was over, that it was truly beyond repair. Wading around in the pool of what-ifs and maybes would eventually cause her to drown. But thinking of the finality of it all was just as suffocating. She had often thought she'd built up their relationship in her head, made it out to be better than it was in moments where missing her had become almost too much to bear. But then she would have a flash or a memory, and she knew it wasn't true. They had been the real deal. Their relationship was woven into the romance novels she read in her down time. The kind that saved lost souls and repaired damaged individuals.

It was there, in the words of cheesy country songs and poems that continued to be quoted years after. It had been real. But it had been wasted on her young and foolish heart. Now, she needed to put it to rest, to allow herself to let it go so that she could move forward. Erica had put it to rest years ago, but she hadn't been as fortunate. The irony of this predicament wasn't lost on Lucy. She had delivered the deathblow to their union, and she was the one left feeling unresolved. The semantics didn't matter after all these years, and she needed the closure.

CHAPTER SEVEN

Erica and Diego sat in the conference room with Sheila and her aunt and uncle, talking about their daughter. Jessica's mother, Beth, was gripping a tissue in her hand as if it was connecting her to this plane of existence. Her father, Roger, was doing his best to remain stoic.

Whenever Erica met with a family under tragic circumstances, she couldn't help but think of her own. Her grandfather had raised her. She had always felt loved and appreciated, but she often wondered if it was a different love than she would have received from her parents. All she remembered of her parents came through anecdotes and pictures. Her mother had died of breast cancer when she was two years old. Her father had left not long after she passed. Her grandfather said he couldn't handle the loss. He had tried, but it had been too much. She'd never heard from him again.

After her grandfather died, she thought about contacting her dad, but the thought was short-lived. Her therapist had suggested there were possibly unresolved feelings or issues, but Erica had never felt like that. She felt like her father's decision to leave her with her grandpa had been done out of love, and it had been the only gift he was capable of giving. There was no need to resolve anything because she never felt as if she was missing out. And, of course, she had the Rodriguez family, who had never let her feel alone.

Diego brought in several bottles of water and set them on the table. "Is there anything else I can get any of you?"

His question was met with silent headshakes.

Erica flipped to a fresh page in her notebook. "Can you tell me why you think Jessica's missing?"

Beth let out a small sob, and Roger put his hand on her leg as he spoke. "Jessica is a good girl. She stays at Sacramento State, Monday through Thursday, then comes home on the weekends to help at the shop."

"Your family owns the bagel shop up on First Street, right?"

Roger nodded. "It's going to be hers one day."

"Has she ever not come home without telling you before?"

Beth's words were drenched with despair. "*Never*. We talk almost every day, and she would've mentioned it. I'd spoken with her on Tuesday, and she said she had a big project to turn in and would see me Thursday night. When she didn't show up on Thursday, I thought maybe she was tired after her project and would be out Friday morning. I tried to call, but her phone was going straight to voice mail, which isn't unlike her, since she's not great about charging it. But when she still hadn't shown up by this morning, I knew something was seriously wrong."

Diego asked, "She has a boyfriend, right?"

"Yes, that's right, and he's driving down here now. He's just as worried as us."

Sheila had been sitting in the corner tapping her foot. "It wasn't him. Can't you put out an APB for her car or something?

Diego stood and started toward the door. "First, I'm going to call the cell company and see if we can identify her last known location. It's a long shot if her phone is off, but it's a starting point. We also need to call Sacramento PD and campus police, and let them know what's happening. At this point, we can't be sure where she went missing."

"Do you know any of her passwords? Social media, email, anything?" Erica asked.

"Can't you get access to that?" Sheila almost yelled.

"Not without a subpoena or search warrant. There are pretty strict laws about this kind of thing. I have no problem trying to get one, but I figured I'd start with the easiest solution." Erica answered in the calmest voice she could muster. Sheila was understandably on edge, frustrated, and scared. But in these situations, a cool head was one of the best weapons you could wield. The calmer you were able to remain, the clearer you could think, and possibilities were all they had at the moment. The emotional disconnect she felt for Sheila in the moment caught her off-guard. She was compartmentalizing the situation, able to see her as a distraught person, as opposed to someone with whom she shared a romantic link. The realization hurt, but not because she wanted to be with Sheila. It hurt because it was apparent this was another dead-end relationship.

Roger pulled a laptop computer out of his bag and put it in front of her. "This is mine, but she uses it sometimes when she's home. You might be able to find something in there."

Erica took the computer and looked at their weary faces. Experiences like this were not only unfathomable for most people but also exhausting. "You should go home and get some rest. I'll call you if we find anything, and if you hear anything, please let us know."

Beth tried to stand, but Roger had to brace her. She was understandably shaken. Sheila put her arms around them both and led them to the door. "I'm going to walk them to the car, but I'd prefer to be here."

The last thing they needed in this situation was to have a civilian, a related one at that, looking over their shoulders. But Erica knew Sheila well enough to know she wasn't going anywhere. When the time was right, she would gently encourage her to go get some rest. She would have been sympathetic to anyone in Sheila's position, but their personal relationship made the emotional part more complicated. "I'm going to start going through the computer."

She sat at her desk and opened the laptop. She opened Facebook first, and luckily, Jessica's log-in was saved. She scrolled through her timeline, but there was nothing out of the ordinary. Next, she checked her messages, but there was nothing that stood out there, either. Finally, she scrolled through the pictures. Jessica and her friends filled the frames, in various stages of playfulness and joyousness. Images of her boyfriend were sprinkled in, and she had to admit, they did look incredibly happy together. There were several pictures of her and her friends at a local Clearbrook bar. She kept scrolling and noticed they frequented the bar at least once a month.

Diego pulled a chair up next to her. "The cell company says the last place they had a ping from her phone was the Sac State campus. I called the Sacramento Police Department and filled them in, and they want to be kept in the loop but don't seem all that concerned." He pointed at the computer screen. "Write down the names of those women tagged in the photos so we can talk to them."

Erica hadn't noticed Sheila back in their workspace until she spoke.

"I've talked to all her friends, and they haven't heard from her either."

Erica finished writing down the names of the three other women who were consistently in every photo. She knew Sheila was trying to be helpful, trying to save them precious time. But her insights into the young women's reactions to Jessica being missing were shrouded with bias. Sheila would want and need to believe they knew nothing. Any other possibility was inconceivable to most people. "I'm sure you have, but we need to do our job too."

She put the notebook in her pocket and moved past Diego toward the door. It was then that she allowed herself to take in the worry and sadness etched on Sheila's face. She stopped in front of her and pulled her into an embrace. Sheila was tense for a moment and then almost collapsed into her arms.

She rubbed her back, trying to soothe her. Erica wished she had words to accompany the gesture, but she couldn't find anything that would bring relief or comfort. She couldn't promise they would get through this together. She didn't have an example from their short history together that she could reference to prove she'd be there for her. So she settled on the only promise she could bring herself to keep. "We're going to find her."

Sheila grabbed her tighter. "Please, you have to. She's all they have."

"We're going to do everything we can." They would do everything in their power to find Jessica. She just hoped they wouldn't be too late. "Go be with your family. I'll call you as soon as we know something."

Erica didn't let herself feel the anger until Sheila was out of sight. Anger toward a man she didn't know how to find, and toward his intentions, of which she wasn't aware. She didn't know if he had Jessica, but just the possibility that he could was infuriating. She was furious he'd dumped poor Claudia Ramos near an abandoned house as though she hadn't mattered.

Whoever this was, had a plan and was a step ahead, at least. There were very few things Erica disliked more than being behind. She allowed herself this moment of anger. She needed it to center her thoughts, to bring everything into focus. Anger had a way of doing that, but the trick was knowing when to put it away or fashion it into something else. In this case, she chose to transform it into determination. She'd get to the bottom of what was going on in her town and hold the bastard accountable.

"So, this is Clearbrook?" Grayson resembled one of those cats suction-cupped to a car window. "It's so much nicer than I imagined."

Lucy let the car roll to a stop and turned on her left blinker. "What were you expecting?"

"I'm not sure, but I think I imagined places along the road where you can tie your horse off while you shop for grain or something."

"What the hell? Did you think there was some time portal on the Five that would take us back to the eighteen hundreds?"

"Don't blame me. That's kind of how you described this place."

"I'm pretty sure I never described a gold rush town." Lucy turned down the familiar street. The small downtown shops hadn't changed much over the years, but that was part of their charm. Although there had been several upgrades since her last visit. There were more parks, more people, but the feel was the same. No matter how long Lucy was away, Clearbrook would always be home. *Home.* She wanted to put off heading to her parents' house for a bit longer. She needed time to relax before being confronted with Erica. She had been able to avoid her before, but talking to her was inevitable this time around, and she wasn't quite ready. "Want to grab some lunch and a drink?"

"Yes, please."

"Okay, there's a place called Junior's right down here. We can sit outside and bring Holly."

It was turning into a beautiful day. The temperature was perfect, and the slight breeze was refreshing. Lucy grabbed Holly and went straight to the back patio of Junior's. Grayson went inside to let the hostess know they had seated themselves on the patio. A few moments later, Grayson emerged, the hostess behind him with a pitcher of water and a small bowl for Holly.

Grayson flipped through the menu. "So, this place what, doubles as a night club?"

Lucy leaned her head back, allowing the sun to seep into her pores. "Something like that. It's a pretty popular bar at night."

"Fancy."

"I swear, you're fueled by snark and wine."

"Don't hate. It's taken years to perfect that formula. So, tell me about your brother."

"Which one?"

"The cop."

"He's a family guy. His wife Melanie is wonderful, and he has two beautiful daughters, Sofia and Gabriela. He plays in a recreation softball league, he likes to—"

"He's about five foot ten? His hair is graying a bit on the sides, and looks like he stays in pretty good shape?"

Lucy's heart caught in her throat. She turned to look inside the restaurant, where Grayson's gaze was fixed. "Holy shit."

"I presume that blond, athletic looking woman with the cop sunglasses on is Erica Chance?"

Lucy felt her stomach tighten and adrenaline flushed her system. *Maybe they won't see us, maybe I can make it to the bathroom, or maybe I should just go back to San Diego.* She kept watching the pair as they talked to the hostess and then moved toward the bar.

"Let's go say hi."

Lucy couldn't turn away. She couldn't move; she was transfixed by Erica. She hadn't thought it was possible, but she was even more beautiful than she had remembered. The pictures she had seen of her over the years on her brother's Facebook page didn't do her any justice. The longing she had felt for the last decade gripped her insides and twisted. They were walking past the window and they stopped. Diego held his hands up around the eyes, looking through the glass. She turned around in her seat to see Grayson waving at them.

"I literally hate you."

He kept smiling and waving, trying not to move his lips. "You'll thank me later."

The door swung open, and Diego opened his arms, inviting an embrace. Lucy went to him and immediately felt a sense of relief. Diego gave hugs like their father. They were warm, tight, and familiar.

"Mom told me you were coming, but I didn't think you'd be here yet."

"We left a day early. I wanted to get to work so I could get back home."

"You work too much."

She put her hands on his face. "Look who's talking."

Diego stepped around her and extended his hand. "I'm Diego."

Lucy was sure Grayson was introducing himself to her brother, but she couldn't hear him. There was a low buzzing sound in her ears, presumably caused by her proximity to Erica. She always thought of Erica as magnetic, and maybe she was right, maybe she actually gave off some sort of frequency Lucy was able to tune in to.

"Hi, Lucy. It's been a long time."

Far too long. Before she could say anything, Erica reached down to greet the dancing dog at her feet.

"What's your name, precious?"

Holly was lapping up every ounce of attention. If she could smile, Lucy thought she would look exactly like she did now. "Her name's Holly."

"Aren't you adorable?"

"She knows it, too."

Erica stood back up, but she had her sunglasses on, making it impossible for Lucy to know what she was thinking. "How have you been?"

How have I been? I have missed you every single day for the last twelve years. I think about what you're doing, whether or not you're happy, who you're dating. "Good, busy. You?"

"Busy, which isn't a good thing in my line of work."

She felt someone come up beside her. "Hi, I'm Grayson."

Erica shook his hand and lifted her sunglasses to the top of her head. "Erica."

There they were, those vibrant blue eyes. They were just as wondrous as Lucy remembered. The only thing that had changed was the small crinkle at their edges.

"Yes, I've heard so much about you." He beamed.

Lucy could've hit him, and she was going to as soon as they got out of here.

Erica laughed. "I'm sure, but almost none of it's true."

Grayson pursed his lips and looked her up and down. "I bet it's all true."

Erica looked confused, and the embarrassment Lucy felt was almost enough to make her knees buckle. Luckily, Diego saved her.

"We have to get going. We have a missing person case to work."

This statement was possibly the only thing that could've forced the gears to switch in Lucy's head. "Missing person? Anything to do with the Claudia Ramos murder?"

Diego pulled his sunglasses out of his front pocket and put them back on. "Easy there, big city reporter. We don't know what this is yet."

His attempt to blow her off wasn't going to distract her. "But could it be?"

The questions were starting to tick off in her head. It was more than a coincidence that there was a murdered woman in this small town and then another missing person within days of each other. She was going to ask another question when an arm came around her waist and a body pressed against her. She knew the smell—vanilla and sunshine. The smell she associated with love, youth, and happiness, and she had never smelled it anywhere but on the neck of Erica Chance.

"It was nice seeing you, Lucy."

It was a brief hug, and it ended about forty years too soon. Erica said good-bye to Holly and Grayson and started toward the car.

Diego kissed her cheek and followed after Erica. "We'll catch up later."

After they were out of sight, she and Grayson sat back down at their table. Emotions popped around her stomach like a pinball machine.

"I see what all the fuss is about."

"Huh?" She was still trying to figure out what just happened. Had Erica just hugged her or was it all a dream?

"Hello?" Grayson snapped his fingers in front of her face. "Earth to Lucy."

"Yeah, what?"

He was waving the menu like a fan in front of his face. "You two are H-O-T hot."

"I wasn't expecting to see her." Of course, that wasn't entirely accurate. Lucy knew she would inevitably run into Erica. What she hadn't been prepared for was the way her body still reacted to her, her desire and need still fervid at Erica's touch.

He sipped his water. "First of all, we need something stronger than this." He put the glass down. "Secondly, that's pretty obvious. Lastly, when are we going to see her again?"

She leaned forward on the table to answer his questions, in order. "Yes, I agree, maybe two or three. Second, I hope it wasn't that obvious, and last, I have no idea."

The server had come over, and he ordered two craft beers. "Well, let's make it happen. How did you survive without me for thirty years?"

She rolled her eyes. She wouldn't give Grayson the satisfaction of telling him how grateful she was to have him here with her.

She looked up at the sky. She needed a moment to take everything in, but all she could picture were Erica's eyes. Her memories no longer did them justice. She had forgotten how blue and vibrant they were. The hue resembled the sky after a storm. Blue at the edges, colliding with gray as you looked closer. Her arms were stronger now, not those belonging to a girl on the threshold of womanhood. Erica was strong, solid, and Lucy had relished the feel of her embrace. Lucy had played out this first encounter dozens, if not hundreds, of times before. The outcomes had held a variety of possibilities, but she hoped for this momentary closeness, among many.

CHAPTER EIGHT

He watched the whole exchange from his car in the parking lot. He knew Erica Chance and Diego Rodriguez were assigned to the Claudia Ramos case. Even if it hadn't been in the newspaper, they were the only two detectives in the whole town. What he didn't know was why they were at his place of employment. He had been meticulous, making sure every angle was covered. So, what had brought them here? Were they trying to run down Claudia's case or did they know Jessica was missing? He'd had her for two days, so it made sense they were beginning to search.

Momentarily, a bit of panic washed over his body, but it quickly gave way to excitement. The chase would be on now, a battle of wits and planning. He reminded himself they'd only been there for a few minutes, and if they'd found anything, they would've been there longer. He was going to need to do something to throw them off his trail, something that could point them in the wrong direction. *Another girl, maybe? It's hard to fight multiple fires on different fronts.* They needed another distraction, and he needed more time with Jessica to make her see how perfect they were for each other. But was it too risky?

He decided he would walk past the patio table, giving the interesting pair of strangers a nod of hello as he moved past them. These two had some sort of connection to the two detectives, which was fascinating. Clearbrook was a town where everyone knew everyone. So where had these two come from? What was the purpose of them being here? Clearbrook wasn't a vacation destination. Sure, they could just be passing through, but it was off the beaten path, too. And why would anyone travel with an obnoxious little dog? The angry little thing growled its disapproval as he passed by, and it took an exercise in restraint not to kick it into the fence.

It wouldn't be too difficult to figure out who they were. He would check their receipt after they closed out their bill. People typically didn't realize just how much information they left behind through their daily tasks. A credit card would give him a first and last name, and if they signed up for a rewards program, he would have an email address and a phone number. After that, he could uncover plenty of personal details. People were creatures of habit, and when they were used to providing so much regularly, asking them to do it again was met without resistance or memory.

He clocked in at the front computer and said hello to the hostess. A pretty little thing, she'd just graduated high school the year before, and she was now attending community college. He'd been able to discover all that simply by listening to her conversations with other staff. He knew the car she drove, who her friends were, and even her favorite food. All the information was there for the taking, for someone who was willing to pay attention, to listen.

It had taken him quite a while to master these skills. Sure, there had been a few missteps along the way, but nothing he would repeat now. He handed the rewards program pamphlet to the hostess. "Make sure you give them one, I don't want you to get in trouble."

She took it from him and let out a sigh of gratitude. "Thanks, I always forget these little things."

"No problem. Be sure to mention the free appetizer they get if they complete it."

She turned and walked toward the patio door. "I will, thanks!"

He wiped down the bar, feeling amused with himself. People, for the most part, were easy to manipulate. You could get almost anything you wanted by assuming you had their trust. That was the human condition after all, wanting to connect, to feel loved, and heard. He had learned long ago how to get what he wanted by moving around people in such a way they hardly noticed they were doing what he wanted them to. And why shouldn't he use his talent to his advantage? He needed to make sure these people wouldn't interfere with his plans. Everyone had a right to protect what belonged to them. Jessica was his now, and he wasn't going to let anything, or anyone, interfere.

CHAPTER NINE

Erica mentally scolded herself once in the car. She shouldn't have touched Lucy, much less hugged her. She wasn't even sure what had come over her. Lucy had seemed just as surprised to see her. Thoughts, memories, and emotions had flooded her system when she stood up in front of her. Erica had tried to treat her like the stranger she was now, but when she started pressing Diego for information, Erica saw the woman she had thought she would spend her life with. Lucy was fierce, tenacious, and relentless when she went after something. It made Erica happy to know that hadn't changed.

"I'm sorry. I forgot to tell you she was coming," Diego said sincerely.

"We've had a lot on our minds."

"Yeah. You okay?"

"It was a long time ago. She's your sister. That's not going to change."

"I just want to be sure. I know she throws you off."

"She used to, but not anymore. I'm okay." *Is that true? Am I okay? Yes, of course I'm okay.* Her feeling of unease had nothing to do with Lucy, and everything to do with the cases they were handling. They were dealing with a murder and a missing person. A missing person case that should technically be handled by uniformed police, not her and Diego, since they had enough on their plates. She was doing it because it was Sheila's cousin, and if she was honest with herself, because gut instinct told her the two were connected. Without any further leads on the Ramos case, though, they were stuck. They'd focus on Jessica and hope it somehow led to a connection. It was weak, and she hated not being more proactive, but everyone they'd talked to hadn't seen anything, and even the video surveillance cameras hadn't given them anything solid. All they had to go on was the time she left Starbucks, and then she'd shown up at the Miller Farm.

"That's the house." Diego pointed cross the street.

"Which friend is this?"

"Heather Henry."

A young woman was sitting on the porch swing when they walked up to the house, and Erica recognized her from the pictures. "Heather?"

"Yeah." Heather didn't look up.

"I'm Detective Chance and this is Detective Rodriguez. We're here about Jessica."

She covered her face and started crying. "You have to find her, please."

Erica sat down next to her. "That's what we're trying to do. What can you tell us?"

She wiped her eyes with the back of her hand, which did nothing to slow the tears from falling off her cheeks and onto her legs. "We've been friends since high school and we would hang out when she came home on weekends."

"Do you go to college?"

"No, I mean yes. I go to community college and I work."

"Okay, when was the last time you talked to her?"

"She called me before she left campus. We made plans to hang out Friday night. She said she would call me when she got to her parents' house, that her phone was going to die, and she had lent her car charger to her boyfriend."

"Was any of this out of the ordinary for Jessica?"

"No, she was terrible with her phone. I don't know how she functions like that. I feel like a piece of me is missing without mine. She said she actually preferred to be without it."

"Did she mention anything about her boyfriend? Were they fighting, had a disagreement?"

"No, nothing like that. Zack is a good guy, and she never complained about him, in general."

"Was there anyone that was making her uncomfortable around campus?"

"Not that she told me."

"Would she have confided in anyone else if something was happening?"

Heather looked at her, appalled. "Do you think she has a stalker?"

"We're just trying to cover all the angles right now."

"Um...I think so. I'm her best friend." She began to cry harder. "What if I missed something?"

"What about when you all hung out here, in Clearbrook? Anything out of the ordinary?" Erica watched Heather's face as she calmed down and looked like she was really considering the question.

Heather leaned forward, resting her elbows on her knees. She took deep breaths, trying to get her emotions under control. "There was a group of guys at Junior's a few weeks ago. They were pretty persistent, but the bartender asked them to leave and they did."

"Were they waiting for you after? Start anything? Say anything?" Diego pressed.

"No. They weren't waiting for us or anything like that. The bartender insisted that we wait for him though, and he walked us out. He kept asking Jessica if she remembered him."

"Did she?"

Heather chewed on the side of her thumb, looking at the ground. "No, she said she didn't."

"Do you remember which bartender it was?" Erica asked.

Heather started crying again. "I'm not sure. It didn't seem like a big deal at the time. Do you think it's a big deal?"

Heather was clearly taking responsibility for her friend's disappearance. Erica wanted to make her understand that regardless of the outcome, none of this was her fault. "No, Heather, it's okay. We just want to make sure we talk to everyone possible."

"Do you remember what he looked like? Anything at all?" Diego asked.

Heather shook her head. "Just a guy, you know? Nothing special or interesting about him. I'm so sorry."

Erica looked at Diego, and he reached in his pocket and pulled out a business card. "If you think of anything else we should know, please call. No matter how small it may seem, we still want to know."

"Okay, I will." She took the card.

"What are you thinking?" Diego sat next to her in the car, running his hand through his hair.

"I don't think it was a group. Groups are rarely involved with a kidnapping unless there's a ransom involved. I also don't think a group of men annoying women at a bar is much of an anomaly, unfortunately. The bartender is interesting."

"Or he was just doing his job."

"That could be entirely possible too. Weird that he kept asking if she remembered him, though."

They headed back to the station. She mentally tried to put pieces together. They had a woman who didn't appear to have an enemy, a stalker, or even a mad boyfriend. She had a good relationship with her family and wasn't prone to erratic behavior. She wasn't heavily tied to social media, so the possibility of meeting someone online was minuscule. All in all, Jessica was an incredibly low risk, as far as a victim was concerned. But yet, here they were, investigating her disappearance. *Just like Claudia Ramos.* She didn't want to make assumptions they couldn't prove, but the similarities were eerie. It was a chilling realization. There was virtually nothing you could do to truly protect yourself from a predator. If they really wanted you, they would find a way to get you. How was she supposed to reconcile that with her line of work? It was like shoveling out a hole in the ground, just to have someone on the other end dumping in dirt. Protecting the innocent was a daunting task, especially when the hunters were so determined. *I just have to be better.*

CHAPTER TEN

Maria Rodriguez shrieked when they came through the door. "Mija!" She rushed over and grabbed Lucy as if she hadn't seen her in six years, as opposed to the five weeks it had been.

"Hi, Mom."

"Miguel, get out here. Our daughter has finally come home." She pushed past Lucy to get to Grayson.

Her father came out from the living room and quickly grabbed her, squeezing tightly. "My little girl."

Lucy always felt like a little girl once inside her father's embrace. The tight protective circle he squeezed her into was one of her most cherished places. She spent many nights wishing to be tucked away inside of it when she'd been reporting in war zones.

A funny looking, white and brown dog poked its head out from behind her dad's leg. It had long, floppy ears; short, stubby little legs; paws that looked like shovels; and a disproportionately large body. Its eyes drooped as it sat down. It looked like it was melting into the ground. Holly struggled to get out of Grayson's arms and ran right over. She bounced around the strange creature, sniffing every inch.

"When did you get a dog? That's a dog, right?"

Her dad reached down and patted its head. "Yes, of course it's a dog. Her name is Bella, but she doesn't belong to us. She's Erica's."

Holly sat next to her, mimicking Bella's pose, minus the melting. "She's Erica's? That's not what I'd expect." She knelt on the floor to get a closer look. Her eyes, although red and droopy, were kind and soft. The giant snout came closer and left a trail of slime as her mouth and nose pushed across her cheek. Lucy couldn't help but laugh at the gesture. "Is she a basset hound?" She immediately liked the dog's disposition. The soft body, lazy sway, and droopy eyes were a sharp contrast to her owner's, which made Lucy like her even more. She thought it strange, yet fitting that Erica would appreciate something so clearly different from herself.

"Yes," answered her mom. "We watch her sometimes, when Erica is at work and can't get away to check on her. Sheila has been doing it for a while, but Erica brought her over this morning on the way to work."

"Who's Sheila?" Grayson and Lucy asked in unison.

"Sheila is Erica's current girlfriend," her dad said.

"Oh?" Lucy was trying to act unfazed by the description, although her stomach dropped and she felt slightly dizzy. She looked at the pictures that had been added to the wall since she last visited. "Have they been together long?"

"I don't think so, but they never are around long." Her dad shrugged and looked at her knowingly.

Her mom interrupted her dad. "Lucy, don't get any ideas. It took Erica a long time to get over you, and I don't want to see her go through that again."

Lucy crossed her arms at the harsh but true accusation. "You know, *I'm* your daughter."

"Yes, of course, Lucy. But Erica is like a daughter to us as well. The daughter that we actually see several times a week."

"That's not fair, Mom."

"Okay, Maria, that's enough. Let's let her get settled in before we start making her feel guilty for never coming home," her dad said.

Thank you, Dad.

"Grayson, last time we visited, you said you collected baseball cards as a kid?"

This was something Lucy never really understood about Grayson. He had a kind of obsession with old baseball memorabilia. The confusing part was that he had no interest in the current happenings of the sport, only the old athletes.

"Yes, I did. I still have quite a few."

Her dad motioned for him to follow him into his office and Grayson followed, Bella and Holly padding happily behind.

"A basset hound still doesn't make sense," Lucy said to her mom.

Her mom put an arm through Lucy's and headed toward the kitchen. "You'll need to ask Erica about how those two came to be. It's a pretty funny story."

"I'm not sure how much talking I'll be doing to Erica while I'm here."

Her mom opened the oven and checked on the enchiladas. The familiar aroma filled the room, and Lucy was taken back to the night her mom had caught her and Erica in a compromising situation.

"You look beautiful," Lucy said as she watched Erica run her hands over the knee length red dress.

"I hate wearing this stupid thing."

Lucy walked up behind her and kissed the back of her bare shoulder. "I know, but it's only for the night. Plus, you really do look beautiful."

"I feel ridiculous. I don't know why we have to go to this stupid thing."

Lucy wrapped her arms around her waist. "It's prom, Chance. You'll regret it if you don't go."

Erica turned in her arms and kissed her forehead. "My only regret will be not getting to go with you."

Lucy felt the same way. She hated the fact that they had dates coming to pick them up. They would spend the evening at the same table, on the same dance floor, going to the same after party, but they wouldn't really be together. "I know. I feel the same way."

"Then let's forget about the stupid prom and go do something, just the two of us."

Erica started kissing her neck, and Lucy felt it in every inch of her body. This was how it always was, every time Erica touched her. Lucy could feel the intensity travel through every nerve ending in her body. "My mom is downstairs," Lucy managed to get out in a heavy breath.

"She's making enchiladas. She isn't coming up here any time soon."

Lucy was trying to calculate the amount of time her mom had been working to prepare dinner, in order to determine exactly how much time they had. She gave in and moved her hand up Erica's leg as she started to pull her toward the bed. The door swung open, and she couldn't move. She saw her mother's shocked expression. The truth was, it would've been nice if it had been just shock that she had seen, but it was disappointment and a bit of disgust.

She pushed Erica backward, forcing her to turn around, to also see who had entered the room. Lucy's mom wiped her hands on her apron and turned away. "You two need to come down. Erica's grandfather is here and dinner will be ready soon." She left the door open and disappeared down the stairs.

Lucy's mouth was dry, her head hurt, and she could barely stand. "What are we going to do?"

"We're going to go downstairs and eat dinner." She took Lucy's hand. "We're going to go to prom and we'll worry about all this tomorrow."

"How can you be so calm?" Lucy thought she might throw up.

"There isn't another option in front of us right now."

"Lucy?" Her mom put the tray on the stovetop.

"Yeah?"

"Did you hear anything I just said?"

Lucy didn't answer because she hadn't been listening, and she hadn't even realized her mom was talking. "Mom, what did you think when you caught Erica and me together?"

Her mother's movement slowed. "Why?"

"I don't know. I was just thinking about it. You didn't talk to either of us for almost a week, and then it seemed like you were just over it. But we never really talked about it."

"I was surprised, and I didn't know what to say. You know, we're Catholics and it was hard for me to wrap my head around." Her mom shifted her weight back and forth, a bit uncomfortable whenever the subjects of Catholicism and Lucy's sexuality were brought up in the same sentence.

"But you did."

Her mom sighed. "Yes, because you're my daughter. What choice did I have?"

"Some parents throw their kids out of the house. Disown them. Hell, sometimes they even kill them."

Her mom stopped her movements and stared at her, her warm eyes reflecting her acceptance and love. "Lucy, you're my only daughter. I just want you to be happy. And to be honest, I thought it might be a phase."

Lucy smiled. "And now?"

"If it is a phase, it's the longest phase I've ever heard of." She laughed.

"Why didn't you talk to me about it? You just said Erica couldn't spend the night anymore." Lucy remembered the conversation quite clearly. Her mom had wrung her hands together through the entirety of what was only about three minutes, but felt like a zillion years. She hadn't been able to make eye contact with her at the time. Lucy knew now that it wasn't out of disappointment, but out of innocence. Her mom wanted to say the right thing, and she wanted to understand. She just didn't have the tools yet.

"I figured you would talk to me when you were ready."

"I wanted to talk to you when Erica and I broke up. I just didn't know what to say."

Her mom put down the bowl she had been drying and took Lucy's hand. "I was heartbroken when I found out. I always found comfort in the fact that at least you were gay with Erica."

She put her hand up, a silent request for Lucy not to interrupt. "I know that's not how it works. If you're gay, you're gay. I didn't understand that yet, but I do now. But when I saw Erica after you two broke up, she was heartbroken. She would burst into tears for no reason; she would spend weeks, sometimes months, away from our house. It was like losing a daughter."

"I'm sorry."

Her mom put her hand over hers. "No, I'm sorry for not reaching out to you. I'm sure you were in pain also. I know it was your decision, and it couldn't have been an easy one to make."

Lucy closed her eyes. "It wasn't."

Her mom patted her hand. "But I meant what I said. It took her a long time to get over you. I've set her up on plenty of dates, but she's very picky."

Lucy felt the shock of the statement roll through her body. "You set her up on dates?"

"Sure! I joined PFLAG and met lots of people just like me. All of whom were more than happy to help me arrange a few meetings between their daughters and Erica."

Lucy had no idea her own mother had been actively working against her all this time. Of course, it wasn't intentional. Lucy had never vocalized her desire to have Erica back. But it stung all the same. Knowing her mom wanted Erica to be with someone else, anyone besides her, burned in her chest. It wasn't logical, this feeling of betrayal. But it was there, all the same. "Let's just talk about something else."

Her mom rolled her eyes. "I'd set you up too, if you ever came home. Now, as I said earlier, we're going over to Diego's house tomorrow for dinner. MJ will be there with his new girlfriend, and you and Grayson are invited."

MJ was Lucy's other brother, the middle child, and forever player of the family. He went through girlfriends like Lucy went through shoes. Lucy also didn't need a reminder of what tomorrow was. There was no possible way for her to forget, even if she wanted to. The date was tattooed on her shoulder. Erica had a matching one on her shoulder with Lucy's birthday, or at least she did.

"It's Erica's birthday," her mom said excitedly.

"I know what day it is, Mom." Lucy let her sarcastic tone highlight her annoyance.

Her mom opened the fridge, pulled out a bottle of wine, and poured some into two glasses. "Don't get an attitude with me. You should come see your brother anyway."

"Does Erica know we're coming?"

"I don't know. I'm sure she'll assume."

"I have a lot of work to do, Mom. We'll see."

"It's always work with you. I'm sure you can carve out two hours to spend with your family. This is why you're still single, Lucy."

"We'll be there." Grayson slid onto the stool next to hers before Lucy had a chance to respond.

Her mom's face lit up. "I'm so glad you came with her, Grayson. Can we do my hair tomorrow morning?"

"Of course we can. Can't go to a party without being fixed up properly."

Lucy shot him a dirty look, which he seemed to revel in. Grayson and her mother continued to chat back and forth as Lucy let her words wash over her. She had used the word "single" like a weapon, a magic bullet meant to pierce her subconscious, to make her aware of her shortcomings. But being single was by choice; it wasn't situational, it was intentional. She had her career, friends, Holly, and she didn't need a significant other to complete her. She was content with casual dating and no complications. But even as she let this practiced self-talk run through her head, she knew it wasn't true. Being single was by choice, yes, but because no one ever measured up to the one person she compared everyone to.

CHAPTER ELEVEN

Erica sat in the squad room alone. She had sent Diego home hours ago and had already called Maria to tell her she'd be late picking up Bella. Maria offered to keep her overnight, and she accepted the offer. She hated leaving Bella overnight, but the Rodriguez house was like her second home and she'd hate to wake up everyone when she was finally finished at work. And she didn't want to run into Lucy. She should examine that feeling, but now wasn't the time. Claudia Ramos was dead and Jessica Vargas was missing, and they deserved her attention right now and nothing else.

There was no hard evidence the two were connected, but she couldn't shake the feeling. They were similar in looks, age, interests, and hometown. Erica didn't believe in coincidences, and she wasn't going to start now. She continued to stare at the two pictures on the board, which each had their separate columns, information listed under each. The longer she stared at them, the more her frustration continued to mount. She was missing something; she just wasn't sure what it was.

The chief had told her and Diego that he wanted this sewn up, with a resolute outcome as soon as humanly possible. He didn't like the idea of his small town being afraid, and that's exactly what these cases were causing. Their phone lines had been flooded for the last few days with questions about Claudia and now Jessica. Parents wanted to know if it was safe to let their daughters go out at night, and there were questions about how close they were to finding Claudia's killer, and if Jessica was dead. *People are scared, and maybe they're right to be.*

"Hey, Chance." Robbie Kern had been with the Clearbrook Police Department for almost thirty years as a uniformed officer, and now he was a volunteer. Everyone knew how hard it was to let go of the badge.

"Hey, Kern. You're here late."

He sat next to her and sipped on his cup of coffee. "Chief asked for volunteers to be here to man the phones, so I took the night shift."

She leaned forward, putting her elbows on her knees and rubbing her head. She had to figure out what she was missing.

"Looks an awful lot like the double murders we saw twenty-five years ago." He crossed his legs and continued to sip his coffee.

"What do you mean?"

"I remember it like it was yesterday. We had two murders in a matter of two weeks here. Angelica Peña and Mariana Cruz, about the same age as the two here." He pointed to the board. "They were about ready to bust the whole world right open, never got the chance though. One went missing. We found her body first, and then the other about two weeks later. Damn shame, really. We spent months trying to crack the case, but we never could. Never caught the guy."

"Do you remember how they were killed?"

"Of course I do. Blunt force trauma to the head. They were cleaned up, put on display."

"I've never heard of these cases." She was split between being angry about not knowing the old case and excited there was something, anything, else they might be able to go on.

"No one talks about it. Dark days around here, knowing there was a murderer out there, living amongst us, not knowing who it was. It was a terrible time and a blemish on our department. We had a few thoughts but were never able to put anything solid together."

"Are the files still here?" She stood, ready to head down to archives, when she heard the dispatch radio. An abandoned car matching Jessica's had been discovered down by the delta.

Kern smiled at her. "Go, I'll grab the files and bring them up here for you."

"Thanks, Kern, I appreciate it."

"No problem, kid."

She thought about calling Diego, but there was no reason to at this point. Tearing him away from his family wasn't necessary for a car. She also thought about calling Jessica's family, but she wanted to assess the situation first.

It only took a few minutes to get to the small restaurant located at the waterway, which served as a natural border for their town. During the late spring and summer, this area would be bustling with boats, jet skis, and a variety of other water sport patrons. But right now, the only other lights in the area came from the police cruiser parked alongside the abandoned car.

Erica left her lights on and walked up to the officer who was jotting down information on a clipboard. He gave her a series of answers before she had the opportunity to ask anything. "Restaurant owner called it in, said he hadn't been here in about four days, so it was left at some point during that time. Plates match the Vargas car."

Lucy slid gloves on, pulled the driver side door open, and sat down in the seat. The officer walked up alongside the open door. She put her hands on the steering wheel and glanced down at the pedals. "Whoever took her left the car here."

"How do you know she was taken?"

She opened the glove box and went through the papers inside. "Jessica Vargas is only five foot three. The seat would've been pulled all the way up, if she had driven it last. This seat is as far back as it goes."

"I already called the tow company. They're on their way."

"Good, I want it taken into the station, and we need to check every inch for prints, fibers, everything." She pushed the trunk latch and walked around to the back of the car. "Have them take pictures of everything." There were bags in the trunk, along with an umbrella and a jacket. This proved, as far as Erica was concerned, that Jessica had been taken. Otherwise she'd have taken the items out of her trunk.

She called Diego and filled him in, and he offered to call and update the family on what they had found. She was grateful for the assistance. She was never very good at that part of the job, whereas Diego had a natural ability to calm people. The tow truck arrived quickly, and Erica watched diligently as the operator hooked up the car, wanting to make sure no evidence could be compromised as he pulled it up onto the back of the truck. She had placed evidence tape over the doors, ensuring they would only be opened upon processing. Nothing could be processed until the next day when the staff came in, but maybe there was something. Whoever had taken Jessica had clearly been in the car, and she hoped they left something behind.

The other police officer pulled in front of the tow truck to escort him back to the station. Erica looked at her watch. It was a little after eleven. She could go back to the station and start going over the old case files, but she'd rather do that with Diego. Two sets of eyes were always better than one, especially in this instance.

She decided the best course of action would be to go home, get some rest, and start back at it the next day. She was just going to make one stop. She wanted to go back to Junior's and observe the staff. Jessica was a regular at the establishment, and it appeared the same was true for Claudia. Maybe if she sat there for a bit as a guest instead of a police officer asking questions, she'd be able to notice something that could help. It would also help take her mind off Lucy, a ghost stirring up all kinds of stuff she wasn't prepared to deal with.

"Your mom's cooking is seriously off the charts." Grayson flopped down on her bed, arms out.

"We ate hours ago."

Holly jumped up on his stomach and turned two circles before lying down in a ball on top of him. "I know, and I still can't get over it. Think I can talk her into sending me home with some?"

Lucy closed her laptop. "I'm sure it would be the highlight of her month."

"Let's go out." He rolled onto his side, widening his eyes at her.

Lucy stroked Bella's head. The giant marshmallow had sat down next to her and flopped her head on her lap. "There's nowhere to *go out* here. Not the way you're used to, anyway."

"I want to experience the local culture." He smiled.

"Ha! That won't take long."

"Come on, Lucky! Please."

She narrowed her eyes at him. "Why did you just call me Lucky?"

He sat up, clearly excited to reveal what he had learned. "I happen to know that was your nickname when you were a kid. Your dad still calls you that when he talks about all your achievements. Did you know he still has every award you ever won hanging in his office? I mean, like, every one. I even saw a participant ribbon for soccer in there."

"Soccer wasn't my thing."

"Yeah, I gathered that because the award said Participant and not First Place."

"I get it."

"It wasn't even a second place ribbon."

"I understand."

"I mean, I could even understand a third place."

She threw the pillow at him. "I'd love to find your off switch one day."

"Oh, honey, get in line." He threw the pillow back. "I know it's your nickname, but he didn't tell me why."

"I shouldn't even tell you after all that."

"But you will because you like the name. I could tell when I said it."

"I was called Lucky Lucy because I was a bit of a klutz growing up. If there was something to trip on, I would. If there was even the slightest chance I'd hit my head on something, you could be sure I'd find a way. I once got so mad at my brother that I tried to throw my doll at him, but it caught on my shirt and I ended up not only ripping my shirt but hitting myself in the head with the doll, too."

His laughter started out quiet and then turned into a deep, full stomach cackle. "It's just so adorable you keep telling these stories like they're past tense."

"I'm not nearly as bad as I used to be."

He blinked at her a few times and started laughing again. "Okay, just today, I watched you walk straight into a glass door because you thought it was a push and not pull."

"That could happen to anyone."

"Then you pulled the door open and hit yourself in the face."

She reached down and stroked Bella's face. "Don't listen to him, Bella." Her tail thumped up and down at the mention of her name.

He was still laughing on the bed when she grabbed a sweatshirt out of her suitcase. "Let's go out and have a drink so I can listen to you make fun of someone besides me."

She wasn't only in search of a distraction. She wanted to use this opportunity to do a bit of work. Diego and Erica had been at Junior's earlier that day because they thought it was a possible link. She had worked with police officers long enough to know they wouldn't just hand out information to the press without purpose. If the murder of Claudia Ramos was tied to the missing person case, she wanted her hands on the information and leads. Even if she had to dig them up herself.

Chapter Twelve

Erica couldn't remember the last time she was in a bar on a Saturday night. Junior's was crowded, people were loud, drunk, and all over the place. Although, if there was an upside, she was grateful for the good cover it created. It was easy to sit in the corner of the bar, sip her beer, and just observe.

It was pretty easy to tell who was there for what reason. She could pinpoint the group of men looking for a quick hookup, as well as the women who were looking for the same interaction. She could tell who was there for a girls' night out, with no intention of going home with anyone but the friends they had come with. Then, there were the people who looked like regulars. They probably came on their own, with the intention of just running into people they knew. The couples were looking to change up their date night routines. Everyone seemed to fit nicely into their little categories. But where did that leave her?

She realized she recognized quite a few people in the bar, because most she had gone to high school with. They had stayed in Clearbrook to raise families or they'd gotten jobs nearby and never left. She wanted to go say hello, almost longing for a normal connection, but then she'd reveal she was there. If the killer was here, in this bar, the last thing she wanted was to draw attention to the fact that a police officer was nearby. No, she needed to stay as incognito as possible. Best-case scenario was that Jessica was still alive and they would be able to find her before it was too late.

She ran her finger up the side of the sweating glass, watching the condensation flow over her finger. It was peculiar, this sudden need to feel a connection. She hadn't felt it for quite some time. Erica was accustomed to being alone, and she rather liked it that way. She was able to come and go as she pleased, and she didn't worry about checking in with anyone. She didn't worry about the late nights she had to work upsetting someone, either. But now, she felt a piece missing she didn't recognize. An emptiness that left her feeling hollow.

Then the air seemed to shift, and she heard Lucy's voice before she saw her. Or maybe it was that she felt her presence, which she'd always been attuned to. Lucy and her friend Grayson walked directly to the bar and ordered. Grayson was busy glancing around, seemingly taking in the atmosphere. Lucy, however, barely looked up. Erica was surprised that after all this time, she still recognized her facial expressions for what they were, a mirror of what she was feeling. Like her, Lucy seemed to be a bit out of place, ill at ease among people they'd both known a billion years ago. Lucy had never been very good at hiding her emotions, and that attribute hadn't changed in their years apart.

It had been twelve years since Lucy had essentially ripped Erica's heart from her chest and left it lying outside her body. When Erica had driven home that night from UC San Diego, she kept touching her chest, surprised there wasn't a physical hole where her fingers touched. After, Erica had forced herself to get out of bed, to go to classes, go to the gym, but it was all done on autopilot. For months, she spent nights hoping the earth would open up and swallow her whole. Her eyes had burned from the ever-present tears that scorched her cheeks and kept a salty flavor on her lips. Her body had felt heavy, making even the most basic movement painful and forced. It remained, unequivocally, the worst time of her life. She hadn't *almost* lost herself during that period of time, she felt as if there was nothing that remained of her. She'd had to rebuild and become a different person altogether.

From the ashes of Lucy's breakup, came a methodical construction of rules Erica had lived by ever since. She gave her love interests four months, and not a day more. Four months was long enough to know whether or not she wanted to create a life with someone, and if it wasn't there, she'd end it. She refused to ever be the Lucy in a relationship, to let someone believe they were her world, when she had no intention of making them the center of her universe.

One of the women she'd dated had asked her what exactly was she was looking for. She wanted to know what Erica defined as the "it" she was always seeking. Erica hadn't known what to say at the time, and she was unprepared to slap a definition on the side of her proverbial Holy Grail. But later, she realized it was actually much simpler than people would expect. She wanted genuine intimacy. Not in the physical sense, though that was wonderful too, but she wanted it in the emotional sense. She wanted someone she could say anything to, share her deepest, darkest, and weirdest thoughts with, and have it be okay. Intimacy meant finding someone that would rather die than intentionally hurt the person they loved. It meant putting someone not only before themselves, but everything and everyone else, as well. She wanted to feel, in the deepest and most secret part of her heart, that they could overcome anything. She didn't want it just as lip service but as something she felt and lived, every day. She wanted to look into someone's eyes and see herself. She wanted the good, the bad, and everything in between. Anything less wasn't something she'd waste her time with.

It had taken Erica two years to recover from Lucy. Two years of therapy, two years of self-examination, two years of asking what-if. And now, here Lucy was again, only fifteen feet away. If anyone had asked Erica a week ago if there were any residual feelings still brewing inside her, she'd have blown off the implication. Until today, when she touched her again, felt her body against her, felt her breath catch at the familiar scent of Lucy's favorite lotion. Lucy didn't look the same as she had the night Erica had driven away from that college campus. Yes, her skin was still smooth, warm, and welcoming. Her lips were still full and her eyes were still the color of a dark roast coffee. But there were lines around her eyes now, small creases from years of laughing. Laughing while they had been apart, someone else's doing. One thing hadn't changed since she last saw her, though. Lucy was still the most beautiful creature Erica had ever seen.

Lucy looked up and caught her eye. Erica's mind was a flurry of questions about why she had come here, what she wanted, and when she'd leave. Yes, she was here to cover a story, but did she actually need to be here to do it? Clearbrook was *her* town now. Lucy had left it and never looked back. She expected the bubbling in her stomach to be anger, frustration, even annoyance, but that's not what was simmering.

She was frustrated that she wanted to ask Lucy a hundred questions. And none of them had to do with anything that would bring Erica a sense of resolution. She wanted to know how she had been, how her job was, and if she was happy. She felt the draw to want to know Lucy again. *But why?* That would only lead to disappointment, to their inevitable parting. It would lead to Erica hurting all over again, and she wasn't sure she could handle losing Lucy twice.

Erica pushed her reflections away as Lucy and Grayson set their glasses down on the table. She wouldn't let Lucy see the effect she apparently still had on her.

Grayson spoke first, taking a moment in between the sips from his tiny red straw. "Hey, Erica, seems a bit like fate meeting you here."

Erica didn't want to like him, but she did. He had an easy way about him, a smooth and friendly voice. "It's the only bar in town, and I'm not an expert on fate, but I don't think this is it."

He crinkled his nose at her. "Spirited...I love it."

"Hi." Lucy's voice was timid, not like the lively girl she had once known better than herself.

"Hey. You two out looking for trouble?" Erica tried her best to keep her tone light, joking.

"Only if your name is trouble." Grayson winked at her.

Damn it, she really did like him. "Not that I don't want to catch up." She almost choked on the lie. "But I'm kind of working."

Grayson looked around. "I need to become a cop. Your job is awesome."

It was clearly the wrong thing to say, because it only seemed to pique Lucy's interest. "You have a lead?"

"No." She wasn't going to divulge anything to a reporter, and their history didn't matter in this situation. There was a dead college student and another one was missing.

"Is this like a stakeout? I always wanted to be on a stakeout. Should we get snacks?" Grayson slid a chair up next to her, still sipping on the tiny straw.

Lucy hadn't once taken her eyes off of Erica. "You think it's someone who works here?"

"I never said that."

Lucy leaned closer and Erica could feel her breath on her face. Her hair fell forward and brushed against Erica's cheek. Erica sipped her beer to keep her mouth busy.

"No, but you were here earlier, and it looked like you were doing an interview. There's only one reason you'd be back, drinking alone."

Erica already knew Lucy was good at her job. It had been a lifetime since they had last spoken, but that didn't mean Erica hadn't kept track of her. She had read her articles, followed her career, and had been proud of her when she had been awarded a Pulitzer. Putting these pieces together wasn't a stretch, not for Lucy.

"Maybe I just felt like having a drink in the only bar in town." She looked between Lucy and Grayson. "Alone."

Grayson leaned across her, speaking to Lucy as if she wasn't there. "I think she wants us to leave."

Lucy had rested her hand next to hers. Erica made sure not to move her fingers, scared of what the contact would do to her resolve. "I like him. He's very intuitive."

Grayson put his arm around her. "Don't forget exceptionally good-looking."

Lucy wasn't deterred. "You know you look less conspicuous sitting here with two people. How about this, everything is off the record."

Erica considered the prospect. On the one hand, Lucy was right, having two people with her did make her presence seem more like a night out with friends, rather than a stakeout. On the other, she wasn't sure she wanted to spend time with Lucy. Claudia's and Jessica's faces flashed in her mind. They were more important than any uncomfortable feeling she was currently having, and if it helped her cover to have two people with her, then so be it. "Okay, but off the record."

Lucy's eyes lit up, the same way they always had when she achieved some form of victory. The familiarity burned the back of her throat, leaving her speechless. Erica had, at one time, aspired to be the person who put that look on Lucy's face. She wanted to make her happy, to be the one to share all of life's ups and downs. Now, all she was to Lucy was a story she might disclose to new lovers. Or maybe she didn't mention her at all. Maybe Lucy had closed that chapter of her life, the chapter where Erica had played the primary character. She didn't want to know the answer.

❖

Lucy took the seat in front of Erica, wanting the gesture to signify her agreement to keep things off the record, making sure she couldn't track Erica's line of sight. She still couldn't believe Erica hadn't dismissed her immediately. Not for the first time, she was grateful for Grayson. He had a way of easing the situation, making things more comfortable.

But now that she was actually sitting in front of her, close enough to touch, she wasn't sure what to say. There hadn't been a day since they parted ways she hadn't thought of Erica, wondered how she was doing. Now she had the chance to ask her and she couldn't form a single sentence. Not a useful or thoughtful one, anyway. "Crazy weather, huh?"

Erica stared at her. "Not really, pretty typical spring."

"How about that rain a few years back?" Grayson joked. "Brutal."

Erica smiled at him and she seemed to relax slightly. "What do you do, Grayson?"

"I perform miracles on hair."

Realization flashed in Erica's expression. "You do Maria's hair, don't you?"

"I do. I used to do it for free, now I want payment in enchiladas. I won't be making any exceptions."

Erica met her eyes, and she wondered if they were having the same memory. *Prom night.* "She makes a mean enchilada."

"So, Chance, I'm going to call you Chance. You seeing anyone?" He chewed on his straw. Lucy felt her face flush. She wanted to know. She had been looking for any indication, and she should've expected Grayson to just come out and ask it, but it caught her off-guard all the same. Yes, her mom had mentioned something about Erica dating, but she couldn't be privy to everything.

Erica looked at him for a long moment, apparently thinking of her response, which shouldn't have taken much consideration. There were only two answers to his question, but the pause made Lucy question whether she wanted to know the answer.

"I see someone, but we don't call it anything official. And, yes, you can call me Chance. Most people do."

There it was. Erica was taken. Lucy's stomach pinched up and her heart hurt a bit. She didn't want to hear the details. "I met Bella."

A slow smile crossed Erica's face. Bella was apparently a safe and welcomed topic. "Your parents watch her for me."

"She's very sweet."

"Don't let her fool you. She's as stubborn as they come, and bossy."

"Well, you'll be happy to know that she's doing just fine. Holly and her hit it off, and when we left they were curled up on my bed together."

Erica looked like she was going to say something, but whatever she was thinking was interrupted by Grayson standing up and offering to buy the next round. And just like that, they were alone at the table together. Lucy stared at Erica's hand on the table, and she wanted so badly to touch it. She wanted to see if her skin was still as soft as she remembered, if it still burned at her touch. Instead, she tightened her grip around her glass. Drops of water slid down the side, cooling her hot skin.

"How's San Diego?"

Another safe subject to discuss, perfect. "It's warm and sunny, lots of traffic though."

"I couldn't live in Southern California. Too many cars, too many people."

Lucy wanted to tell her that she already knew that. She hadn't forgotten Erica's adversity to any type of city life, to having to deal with traffic on a daily basis. She hadn't forgotten the late-night conversations that she now clung to when she tried to fall asleep. The way those memories were like blankets of warmth and safety that she laid out across her body when she needed them the most. "I know."

Grayson was back, drinks masterfully balanced between his fingertips. He nudged Erica. "Bogey, two o'clock."

"Bogey? I don't think that means what you think it does."

Grayson put his hand on his hip and moved his head in the direction of the bar, eyes widening. "That woman over there seems pretty drunk, and the bartender is paying very close attention."

Erica pulled her phone from her back pocket and slyly took a picture. Then she pulled a small notepad out and jotted down the time. "Thanks."

Grayson, thoroughly pleased with himself, had a smug smile plastered on his face. "I'm clearly a natural."

Erica stood, tracking someone with her gaze. "She's going to the bathroom. I'm going to make sure nothing happens." She was gone a moment later.

Grayson got in her seat and slid closer. "Okay, the chemistry between you two is off the charts."

"What? You heard her. She's seeing someone."

"I don't care what she said. There's fire with you two. And from the way she made it sound, it's nothing serious."

She knew what he meant, because she could feel it, too. She just wasn't sure if Erica reciprocated the feelings. "I don't know."

Grayson rolled his eyes as he sipped on his drink.

"She looks great." Lucy hadn't meant to say it aloud. It was just so apparent that it seemed to jump from her mouth.

"Mmm-hmm. What are you going to do about it, is the question."

"I'm not going to do anything. I'm going to do what I came here to do, my job. When that's done, I'm going to go back to San Diego. And she'll stay in Clearbrook. Worlds apart."

"Lesbians, always making things more difficult than they need to be." He snorted.

"You don't get it."

"What's there to get? You two broke up, there's clearly still something there, so work it out."

"We didn't just break up, I broke her heart." She felt dirty even saying it.

"She'll forgive you."

"No. She won't, not the Erica I knew."

"People change."

"Not fundamentally." One of the things Lucy had always appreciated most about Erica was her loyalty. If she cared about you, there was nothing she wouldn't do. She was fierce in her love for others, a rare quality that was seldom replicated. Lucy knew she had broken that loyalty, that trust. People like Erica didn't hand out second chances.

"I guess we'll see."

"I'm not sure I want to see."

"Don't be dramatic."

"Don't you mean realistic?"

"No, I meant dramatic. What do you have to lose?"

"You mean besides my self-respect and pride?"

"Oh, sweetie, we can make those things disappear with a few glasses of wine. May as well risk it on true love."

Was Grayson, right? *Well, besides the wine thing.* Was there something there to salvage? Was it possible that Erica would be open to trying again? Those weren't the questions that needed to be acknowledged. The only question that mattered was, was she brave enough to try? Could she put it all out there, bare her soul and deal with whatever her reaction was? Her therapist would tell her yes, she was brave enough. She would tell her that she needed this closure one way or another. That knowing, even if it was an ugly and agonizing truth, was better than not.

CHAPTER THIRTEEN

Erica Chance, so smug and arrogant. Sitting in his bar as if he wouldn't notice. He found it almost comical that she believed she could saunter in here unnoticed. She never came in alone, and hardly ever came in with other people. As if he could've gotten to where he was by being stupid, careless. And now, she followed the drunk girl to the bathroom. Some deranged knight in shining armor complex. How wrong she was. He wouldn't pick such an easy and obvious woman. Where would the fun be? Yes, he had seen both Claudia and Jessica at the bar. But everyone in this town, at some point or another, had been inside Junior's. He wasn't a fool, and he'd waited until he found Claudia at Starbucks. Well, "found" was a rather loose word. He knew the route she ran; he heard her describing it to her friends. Then it was just a matter of waiting.

These small-town cops weren't smart enough to connect those dots. They would chase their tails, trying to put pieces together that couldn't be traced. There were dozens of regulars that frequented Junior's. It could be any number of people if that was the direction they were headed. He had a front row seat to their thought process, and he liked watching them flounder. As soon as they started pulling people in from Junior's for questioning, he would take Jessica and disappear. They didn't find him the first time he'd left this town, and this time would be no different.

No matter. She wouldn't find what she was looking for. It didn't matter how many bathrooms she lingered around. He had already taken the necessary steps to throw the detectives off his trail. It would only be a matter of time before they found her, giving him more time with Jessica.

Teresa Ortiz had never really been on his radar, not until he needed a distraction, that is. It hadn't taken much convincing. It never really did. Women were predictable. They had very specific triggers, and babies were one of them. The ruse was simple; he had a car seat with a fake doll in his backseat. He would park next to his intended victim and struggle with the car seat. He would ask for help, and most women jumped at the opportunity. They would bend over the car seat, already half in the car, and by the time they realized it was a fake baby, he'd already have the chloroform over their mouths.

He would take them back to the farm and go back for their cars. No one ever gave him a second look since he had the keys. He would hang on to the car for a few days or get rid of it when he saw fit. He liked to make sure there was no evidence left behind, no way to track him. Plus, he liked being in control of when and where the police came upon their evidence. This was the best way to ensure he was in charge of all aspects. He hadn't had time to go back for Jessica's car, something he regretted. But he had her, and that's what mattered most. In the best cases, there would be no car to worry about, like with Claudia. *Claudia.* He'd had high expectations for that one, just to be let down.

Erica walked past him, back to her table. *Didn't find anything, Detective?* He smiled to himself. That was the problem with the police, they thought they were smarter than everyone else. They wouldn't be able to get ahead of him, and if they got close, he would just disappear again. They were easily distracted. Not like him. He had one clear objective, and no one would push him off course. In a few hours, he would be right back on that track, back with Jessica. Hopefully, she had some time to think about her behavior and was now ready to be a bit more ladylike.

He almost punched the computer screen thinking about their last encounter. He had dragged Teresa down below the barn so he could prepare her for presentation. Jessica had started wailing like a banshee, not only distracting him but making his skin crawl. He hated the emotional cries of women; they were like nails on a chalkboard. He hadn't even waited for Teresa to awaken before taking the hammer to her head. If Teresa had been awake, she'd have fueled Jessica's cries, and he didn't want to deal with it.

Instead, he taped Jessica's mouth and let the blood from Teresa's skull splash her face. Upon impact, the blood had covered her eyes, dripping down her lovely cheeks. When it fell upon Jessica's lips, it was the most beautiful thing he had ever seen. The shock and horror that gripped her face, choking her sobs, and blinding her humanity, were breathtaking. He did it as a warning of what could happen if she didn't comply. He wanted her to see how special she really was to him. He saved her, not only from herself, but from the demise he would serve to her if she didn't give him what he wanted.

He was caught up in the memory when the man who had been with the detective was in front of him, ordering drinks. The stark contrast between his life at the farmhouse and his life here, in the world, warmed him. If he had been younger, it would've made him hard. The adrenaline of maintaining the mask he had created was exhilarating. But he had learned to control those impulses years ago. Now, he had the ability to channel what he wanted the world to perceive versus what he craved. He nodded and gave the order to the other bartender on duty.

Chapter Fourteen

Diego put the small cupcake down on her desk. He smiled, knowing it would be Erica's favorite. Her favorite was absolutely any pastry Diego's wife made. She rubbed her hands together, her mouth already watering.

"You look just like my daughter when I put a cupcake in front of her."

She picked it up and ate half in one bite. She closed her eyes and let the chocolate and strawberry mixture wash through her mouth. "Your daughter is a smart girl."

"Happy birthday, Chance." He leaned down and hugged her.

"Thank you." She shoved the other half in her mouth and licked her fingers. "I just want you to know, if you and Melanie ever divorce, I'm keeping her."

"And here I thought loyalty was your best attribute."

"I'm very loyal, to these cupcakes."

"Did you notice anything at the bar last night?"

"Nothing blatant, but I just can't shake the feeling that we're on the right track with the bar. It has something to do with it. I'm just not sure what yet." She didn't want to tell him about being there with Lucy. Not because it would have bothered him but because she didn't want to answer any questions. She also didn't have the desire to do any self-reflection at the moment. She hadn't expected to be transfixed on the similarities and differences between the girl she had once known and the woman Lucy had become. Lucy had always been intuitive, with good instincts. She had clearly honed those skills over the last several years, and had chosen the right career. But in brief moments, Erica still caught glimpses of the young woman she had loved fiercely. It was the way Lucy's face would flush when she caught Erica looking at her. The way she had left her hand so close, an unconscious gesture to anyone watching. But it wasn't unconscious; it was something they had done before they came out to their families. The need to be close when eyes were watching. *Or maybe I'm just reading too much into it.*

He grabbed the files from her desk and started flipping through them. "Did you find anything of interest in here?"

She had been so caught up in the cupcake, she had almost forgotten about the case files. She wiped her hands on her pants and walked over to the board. "Yes, pretty much everything. Did you bring any more of those?" She looked at his desk, in search of more cupcakes.

"There will be more at dinner tonight. What did you find?"

She started writing as she talked. "Both victims in the old cases were college-age women, Latina, close to their families, good grades. One went missing from a parking lot after a movie with friends, the other was last seen at a clothing store. They were both missing for several days before a body was found. Both had been killed by blunt force trauma, both cleaned up, and left at a rural farm house."

"Were there any leads?" Diego had stopped flipping through the files and was listening.

"Everyone was a suspect back then. They brought in everyone for questioning, from the store clerk to visiting cousins. But there was no physical evidence, there were no leads, and no one could think of anyone who would want them dead."

Diego rubbed his face. "So, we're in no better position now than they were twenty-five years ago."

"Well, comparing all the autopsy reports, we might have something. All three women were struck in the head, the murder weapon appears to be a hammer, and the coroner suspects the murderer is right-handed. Also, we think we know what trophy he takes after he kills them. Each of the women had their left earring removed. I didn't think anything of it when we found Claudia, but the same earring was missing on Mariana Cruz and Angelica Peña."

"So, what, this guy has a thing for jewelry?" Diego looked over her shoulder and smiled.

"Three victims? You realize that means serial killer."

The familiar voice smacked Erica in the back. It pushed against her, the strain of desire mixed with a need for self-preservation pulling her in different directions.

So she did the only thing she could, she made a joke. "Jesus, you'd think the security in a police station would be a little stricter. They'll let anyone in." She turned around.

Lucy had her arms crossed over her chest, her hair pulled back in a loose ponytail. She wore a tank top, and there was a large scar on her right arm that hadn't been there twelve years ago. Erica fought back the urge to ask what happened.

Lucy pushed a strand of her dark brown hair out of her eyes, tucking it behind her ear. "Security? You do realize we went to school with pretty much everyone in this building." She smiled slightly. "Now, about your serial killer…"

Her accuracy was annoying. "You can't report that. You weren't even supposed to hear it." Lucy might be able to come and go as she pleased anywhere in her town, but Erica wasn't going to let a reporter, any reporter, publish anything to put this case in jeopardy. Not while Jessica was still missing. It was too risky.

"But you do think they were all done by the same guy?"

"Or woman," Diego added. "We don't have any suspects yet."

Lucy snorted. "Unlikely. Women only make up seven percent of all serial killers, and when they do kill, it's almost always through poison. Not only that, the vast majority of female serial killers usually fall into one of four categories: Angels of Death, Black Widows, Munchausen's, or post-partum killings. It's very unlikely they would be targeting college age women."

Diego stared at her for a long moment before saying anything. "I don't know whether to be impressed or worried about you."

She walked closer to the case board, seemingly mesmerized. "I have a thing for true crime novels. And you seem to forget that I cover the criminal beat in San Diego."

Erica was caught off guard by Lucy's comfortable ease in their meeting space. Did she not have any boundaries? "You still can't be in here. This is an open investigation."

"I know." She kept looking at the board. "Are you sending out the samples from the earlier victims, to check for DNA evidence?"

Erica crossed her arms and shifted her weight. "Lucy, you can't be in here."

"Yes, I can."

The absolute gall of this woman was astounding. Erica's neck burned with anger, but she fought the urge to argue with her. "No…you can't."

Lucy turned and faced her now. The sneaky smile that used to send Erica over the edge crossed her lips. "I ran into the chief this morning at the bagel shop. I explained to him how much experience I had doing investigative reporting in San Diego. He thought since there were only two of you, I could be of some assistance."

What? Erica walked over to her desk and grabbed her cell phone to call the chief and put an end to this.

"I'm not going to get in the way. I'm just going to observe, help where I can, and I get the exclusive. You won't even know I'm here."

Erica held the phone up to her ear, and she was relieved to see it wasn't shaking.

"Think of me like a consultant." Her voice held the tone of promise and a bit of determination. She emphasized it with an innocent smile.

Erica turned her back on the rehearsed proposal. It only took a few rings before the chief answered her call. But before she could even get her objection out, he derailed her hopes of keeping Lucy away.

"I know why you're calling, Chance, and there's no need to protest. Lucy is going to help. She's seen and reported on dozens of cases like this and we haven't, which means she'll be a good set of eyes to have around. She's going to help, so keep her safe. I have to go. We're on the fourteenth hole." She turned around to find Lucy shoving a cupcake in her mouth. *Her* cupcakes, that Diego had told her she needed to wait for.

"These are really good." She kept chewing. "Oh, happy birthday."

Diego shrugged, looking guilty. "I had one more and she's my sister."

Lucy still had chocolate on her lips, and she swallowed hard. "Yikes. Was this yours?"

"It's fine." She was irritated Lucy had inserted herself into her world so easily, irritated that she ate her cupcake, but mostly irritated that she still found her utterly adorable. "You're going to consult, there's nothing I can do about that, but you need to stay out of our way. It's for your own safety."

She nodded and then, like Erica, wiped her hands on her jeans. "I hear what you're saying, but I'm not going to do that. Is there any milk?" She waved her thought away. "I'm going to be with you every step of the way. This may be the biggest story Clearbrook has ever seen, and if it's a serial killer case, I'm not going to miss the chance to report on it."

Erica clicked the whiteboard marker cap in her hand. "These are people, Lucy. People are dead and people are missing. It's not just some story."

"Yeah, and that happens whether I report on it or not. So I choose to report, make sure people know these victims. I make sure their stories are remembered and heard."

Erica understood what Lucy was saying, and she could appreciate the need for the public to know what happened and remember the victims. Erica knew Lucy would do the women justice, and it was better to have the story told with facts rather than assumptions. The unnerving aspect was having Lucy around every day until the completion of the case. Lucy was not only ignoring how this might affect her, she didn't seem to care at all. Lucy was still driven by selfish aspirations, discounting the feelings of everyone she would impact. *Just like old times.*

❖

The look of anger in Erica's eyes was unnerving. It wasn't Lucy's intention to upset her, but she had meant what she said. This story needed to be told and she was going to be the one to do it. Still, she didn't like upsetting Erica, and she needed to prove she could be helpful.

Erica headed toward the door. "Let's go down for processing."

Diego got up and followed Erica, flashing Lucy an apologetic look as he passed. Lucy banged her foot into the desk and caused a cup full of pens to fall to the ground. She tried to catch it on the way down, but she hit the cup and caused the pens to spread farther than they would've once they hit the ground if she'd just let them fall. She immediately bent down and started picking the pens up, shoving them back into the cup as she mentally berated herself for being so clumsy. *So much for helpful. Nice start.*

Erica was beside her, helping. "Lucky Lucy, some things never change."

They went for the last pen at the same moment, and their hands touched. The contact caught Lucy off guard, and she went to stand and hit her head on the desk.

Erica laughed. "You should take your show on the road."

Lucy put the cup back on the desk, harder than she had intended. "It's always been my plan B."

"Let's just hope your investigative reporter skills are more honed than your basic ability to move around a room."

"I can hold my own. Don't worry about me." She knew Erica had been joking, but it was really important that Erica believe she was good at her job. She pushed past her to catch up with her brother. She wanted to put the moment of embarrassment behind her. But she didn't miss the old nickname Erica had used with almost a sense of nostalgia.

The processing area was little more than a three-car garage in size. There were several tools hanging from pegboards, a jack, several portable lights, and a wall filled with gloves, evidence bags, and clipboards. There was also a large workbench area and a desk with a computer. Lucy bit back her comment about this being more like a mechanic shop than an evidence-processing center. She didn't want to seem arrogant or condescending. She wanted Diego and Erica to look at her as someone who was trying to help, not belittle their work. It certainly made her appreciate the resources available in the big city, though.

A rather petite woman dressed in coveralls hopped out of the front seat of the car. She wore a navy blue hat that read Clearbrook Police on the front in gold, her light hair had been pulled through the hole in the back, and she wore goggles and gloves. She had a fingerprint dusting brush in her hand, which she dropped in her front chest pocket when she noticed the three of them.

"Hey, Chance." The short woman's tone was a little too seductive for Lucy's taste.

"Hey, Stein. You got anything for us?"

She stared at Lucy while speaking to Erica. "Straight to the point today, huh?"

Diego, who was probably unaware of whatever flirtation was between Erica and this other woman, wasn't in the mood today. "We have a missing person, Stein."

Stein pointed over to the desk. "I bagged everything I found in the car, but there was no blood, no signs of a struggle. I haven't even found a fingerprint."

"Not even one of Jessica's?" Lucy asked before her brain told her to stop.

Stein squinted at Lucy. "No, I haven't found a single one. Whoever drove this car wiped everything down thoroughly. I did find her cell phone. It's on the counter, but the battery is dead."

Erica pushed on the bridge of her nose. "We need to send everything out for processing anyway. We need to make sure we cover every angle." She grabbed the bagged phone from the counter. "Thanks, Stein."

"Anything for you, Chance." She slid back into the car.

Lucy thought they would go back to the office, but they started toward the cars instead. "How long does it take to send items out for processing?" In San Diego, she knew the police department could put in a rush order and get things back within seventy-two hours.

Diego looked disappointed when he answered. "Usually about a week."

"A week?"

"Yeah, we don't have our own processing center." He motioned at the station. "We have to send things out to private or state-sponsored agencies."

"It could be too late in a week."

Erica pulled the car door open and leaned against it, staring at Lucy as she went to get into the backseat. "You don't think we know that? Look, this isn't San Diego, but we do our best. We're going to find Jessica and catch this guy with good old-fashioned police work."

"Okay." Lucy slid into the car and held up her hands placatingly, not wanting to piss anyone off. "Where are we going now?"

"To my house," Erica said as she put on her sunglasses and rolled down the window.

Lucy was going to ask why, since it didn't make any sense, but Erica and Diego knew what they were doing.

CHAPTER FIFTEEN

When Erica opened the door, it only took a few moments for Bella to come wobbling toward her. Maria had texted her earlier, letting her know she had dropped Bella off after a full breakfast of eggs and bacon. It didn't matter how many times she asked Maria not to feed Bella that kind of food, Maria always spoiled the dog rotten.

Much to Erica's surprise, Bella scampered right by her and went straight to Lucy.

The shock must have shown on her face because Lucy laughed. "Don't be offended. I'm just new to her. Holly does the same thing."

Diego walked straight over to the computer and powered it up. Erica handed him the phone and he plugged it in.

"Why are we doing this here?" Lucy asked, and she started walking down the halls, looking around.

"Our IT guy only works four days a week, and we have to pay him overtime to come in on a weekend. We'll scan it here first, and if there is anything we can't figure out, we'll pay for him."

She couldn't hear what Lucy said under her breath, but Erica was pretty sure it was a mocking comment about the size of their small department. Another reminder that Lucy had moved on from their small town. San Diego was now her home, and she had outgrown Clearbrook. "Can I get you something to drink?"

"Sure, do you have any tea?" she called from one of the back bedrooms.

"Yeah, it's in the fridge. Help yourself."

Lucy walked by a few moments later. "Such a fine hostess."

"You're not a guest." Erica stared at the iPhone, willing it to turn on now that it had a power source. The home screen lit up a few moments later.

Diego had Jessica's Facebook account open on the computer, and when the password entry screen popped up, she looked at him. If they couldn't figure it out, they would need to go back to the station and get her father's computer. She silently cursed herself for such a rookie move, especially with Lucy watching. Diego read out the anniversary of her and her boyfriend. Erica typed in the numbers, but they weren't correct. Next, she tried Jessica's birthday, still wrong.

Lucy leaned over Diego's shoulder, grabbed the mouse from his hand, and started scrolling through her pictures. She came upon a small orange cat, who, as it turned out, had his own album on Facebook. She clicked on the picture and read the name aloud. "Julius." She pointed to the phone and Erica punched in the numbers that matched the name. It opened.

Lucy shrugged and took a swig of her iced tea. "Most people like their pets way more than any human they know."

Erica glanced down at Bella who had curled up in a large ball at her feet. Her neck rolls were falling over her collar, and there were deep snores coming from her snout, which was pressed against her foot. "I can see that." She tried her best to wish away the redness that she felt burning in her cheeks. It was embarrassment, not anger she felt. They were the detectives, but it was Lucy who had figured out the password.

Diego opened several programs on the computer and dialog boxes started opening, indicating they were screening and downloading the contents on the phone.

"You're allowed to do all this on your own computer? Isn't this evidence?" Lucy asked, now wedged between her and Diego on a stool she had dragged over from the breakfast bar.

"Diego and I both have computers at home, purchased by the police department. We can access the department network from here with a virtual pin. Since we're the only two detectives, the chief wanted us to have home access too. These also happen to be faster than the ones we have back at the office."

Diego snorted. "She makes it sound real nice. He got us these computers so we would work from home and be less likely to put in official overtime."

He wasn't wrong; the chief would save a buck wherever and whenever he could. Even if that meant buying them both an expensive computer system, paying for it upfront, and then letting it pay for itself.

Erica was flipping through the contents of Jessica's phone, but there was truly nothing out of the ordinary. She didn't make a lot of phone calls, and the incoming and outgoing were all marked with recognizable names, same with the text messages. The pictures in her phone were nothing exciting either. "When those pictures are done uploading, we'll take a closer look."

Erica needed to move around. She thought better that way. Lucy moved past her a moment later, walking toward the wall of photographs. Lucy stared at them for a long time with her hand on her mouth, an indication she was deep in thought.

"You're more a part of my family than I am," she said, only above a whisper.

Erica looked at the photos, and from first glance, Lucy's statement would be true. The sadness in Lucy's voice scratched at the inside of her chest. She had no idea how often her family spoke of her, how proud they were of her, and just how much they missed her. "No, they miss you."

Lucy's cheeks flushed red, and she bit on her thumbnail for a moment. "Are they the only ones?"

Erica wasn't sure what to say. She did her best not to think about Lucy at all, but was that effective? Had it actually worked? She knew the answer was no. She still thought about Lucy every day. The pain had just become easier to bear. But would she admit that out loud to the woman who had broken her?

She looked at the wall and pointed to a picture of two twelve-year-old girls. They were in the thralls of summer, mouths covered in ice cream, hair damp from the pool, towels wrapped around their skinny bodies, which neither of them had grown into yet. "I miss those two."

"Yeah, me too." Lucy had a curious look on her face.

Erica looked back at the picture, feeling suddenly sad. "Everything was so much easier back then."

"When we were twelve? Yeah, I'd say so." She laughed a little. "They aren't gone. They just grew up."

Erica's phone buzzed in her pocket, and when she saw the familiar name, she felt the need to turn from Lucy. She felt a bit raw and unbalanced. A small part of her had opened up, looking at the pictures and hearing Lucy's words. Surprisingly, she had wanted the conversation to continue. But her caller reminded her that there were more important issues at hand. "Hey, Sheila."

"Have you found anything?"

"Actually, can you come over? We have her phone and are about ready to go through the pictures. You could probably be a big help."

"I'll be right there."

She glanced over at Lucy, who seemed a bit disappointed at the invitation. That wasn't Erica's intention, but she felt it was necessary all the same. Any bit of help was welcomed at this point. She couldn't sacrifice that for Lucy's benefit, or her own. She briefly thought of going back over, saying something, anything, but the moment had passed.

CHAPTER SIXTEEN

Had that just been a moment between her and Erica? She wanted to call Grayson and go over each detail for his examination. She was just thinking about slipping out the door to call him discreetly when she heard a car door close. A few moments later, Sheila walked through the front door. She didn't knock, the doorbell didn't ring, and the familiarity stung more than Lucy could have expected. She knew Erica was seeing someone, but she hadn't anticipated having to see that someone.

Sheila went straight to Erica and threw her arms around her, burying her face in Erica's shoulder. Erica kissed her cheek and mumbled something. Lucy should've been able to hear the exchange, she was standing close enough, but a buzzing had started in her ears and was now throbbing in her head.

Lucy couldn't will her feet to move, and couldn't take her eyes off Erica's hand resting on the small of Sheila's back. She felt dizzy and painfully out of place. Erica guided her toward the computer to look at the pictures on the screen. It wasn't that any of these actions were all that significant; there was no passionate kiss, no exchanges of devotion, but it was the ease in which they touched. The way Sheila gripped Erica's arm as Diego flipped through the images was so...natural.

Lucy had done a bit of reconnaissance when she had first learned of Sheila. She told herself it wasn't because she cared who

Erica was dating, but because she was interested in all aspects of the investigation. It seemed very reasonable at the time, and still did. She knew Sheila wasn't from Clearbrook, but a few members of her extended family were. She had moved to the area when she was eighteen. *Facebook is a useful tool, even if that did make me feel like a stalker.* But the rest was a bit of a mystery. She kept everything on social media private, and a basic Google search didn't turn up anything of interest. She briefly toyed with the idea of running an extensive background check but talked herself out of it. She was worried Sheila would turn out to be exactly as she appeared, and then Lucy would have to give her the benefit of the doubt.

Lucy started planning her escape. But she couldn't, not after she made that big show of being able to help, of being an asset. *Shit.* She needed to sit down, and luckily, the couch was only a few steps away. She fell back onto it, and almost immediately, Bella was up next to her, head on her lap. She tried to send the large dog subliminal messages, hoping she could help her make sense of all these jumbled emotions. Bella stared at her for several seconds, and Lucy thought maybe it had worked. Then she yawned, let out a long breath, and put her head back down. *Helpful.*

Lucy pulled herself out of her own self-pity, only because Sheila had apparently recognized something in the photos. "That's Lance Wilds. They used to date. The breakup wasn't a good one. He called her all the time and followed her around for a while. It was bad. But they've been broken up for a while now."

Erica rubbed her back. "That's good. We'll go talk to him."

"I'm sorry. I forgot to wish you a happy birthday."

Erica touched her face. "I think you get a pass. You've had a lot on your mind."

"Do you want me to come over tonight? I can make you dinner."

"No, go be with your family. I'll call you if we find out anything else."

Apparently, Sheila hadn't realized Lucy was sitting in the room until she stood to leave. She looked her over for a long moment, probably trying to place her. "You're Lucy, right?"

"Yes, Lucy Rodriguez. I'm very sorry about your cousin." Lucy stood to shake her hand. She hoped the smile she plastered on her face hid her feelings of unease.

"You're Diego's sister."

"Yes."

"So, then you're also…" She looked over at Erica, who was now awkwardly pretending not to listen.

Lucy knew what she was thinking. "Yes, I'm also that Lucy."

She expected to see a bit of anger on Sheila's face, maybe a flash of jealousy. But it was nothing like that. Her eyes only showed the glimmer of recognition and something else, sadness.

"It's nice to meet you, Lucy. I'm Sheila, a friend of Erica's."

"Nice to meet you too." Lucy wanted to take this chance, ask her for an opportunity to sit down and talk about Jessica. She wanted to get a family member's perspective on having a missing cousin, in the shadow of a murdered woman. A woman with whom her cousin shared numerous attributes. But she also didn't want to cause more panic, or imply that the two were connected for certain. Usually, it wouldn't have bothered her because the scent of the story would have pushed her past any semblance of appropriateness. But that approach would upset Erica, and that was the last thing she wanted to do. Not only because she wanted to stay on this case for an inside look at whatever was happening in Clearbrook. But also because the thought of upsetting Erica was more than she thought she could bear right now.

Sheila stared at her for another moment before leaving. She wasn't sure what she had expected. Maybe for Sheila to be a bit crasser, or even aloof toward her. But that wasn't the case, Sheila had looked at her with recognition and acceptance. But what did that mean?

There was no time for further reflection, not now anyway. They were on their way to go talk to Lance Wilds. She watched as Erica kissed Bella on the head, getting a tail thump of recognition.

There had been a wide range of emotions over the last several minutes. Lucy's head was swimming with the meaning of it all. She felt suddenly tired, and her head felt heavy. Following a potential lead was a welcome relief. At least this was something she could follow, something she understood.

Chapter Seventeen

Jessica?"

He wiped the hair from her eyes. She had fallen asleep, despite the filth and sweat. It had been a fitful slumber at best, and she shuddered and fought in her dreamland. He liked to think she was dreaming of him, just as he had dreamt of her.

"Jessica?" He touched her face more forcefully and she jostled herself awake. It took her a moment to realize where she was, and the panic in her eyes was evident. "Yes. You're still here."

He pulled the tape from her mouth in one swift, quick motion. Then he pulled out his pocketknife, turning it over in his hand, the motion forcing her to gulp audibly. He pushed her forward, forcing her body to bend in half. He pulled up her hands and used the knife to cut the zip ties free. The look on her face was part terror and part gratitude. He wasn't sure which he enjoyed seeing more.

"If you behave, there will be no need for the tape or ties."

She nodded her understanding. She put her hand up to her throat and rubbed the skin. "Water?" Her voice was dry and crackling, like it had been stepped on.

He handed her a bottle of water and she gulped it down, not taking a moment to catch her breath. He reached behind his back and grabbed a white bag with grease stains seeping through. He handed her two hamburgers and an order of French fries. She tore the wrapper open and shoveled the food into her mouth, barely chewing.

He tried then to touch her, more gently this time. He was, after all, the one who saved her from the hunger pains. When she still recoiled at his touch, he grabbed her face and squeezed. Her face started to grow red where his fingers touched her skin, and he squeezed harder, wondering if he could actually witness the transformation to bruising. He shoved her face away before he could see his theory at work. He didn't want to fall down the rabbit hole of watching the body react to intentional infliction. He wanted this time to be different; he wanted it to last forever.

"Can I have more water?"

Initially, he was caught off guard by her request. The others hadn't been brazen enough to ask him for anything, but then, she wasn't like the rest of them. "Yes." He handed her the bottle.

"Thank you."

"I'm glad you're here."

Her eyes flashed with confusion and anger, but she managed to temper them after only a moment. Someone else might not have noticed, but he did. He knew where to look to see the truth in someone's soul peeking through. But this was hopeful. Jessica wanted to comply, even if her emotions temporarily betrayed her at the moment.

"Thank you for having me."

It wasn't sincere and he was angry at her lie, but he appreciated her trying all the same. It would just take time for her to feel more secure in their relationship. She'd come around, and he didn't care how long it took. He sat down next to her, letting his shoulder brush against hers. She froze for a moment, and he fought the urge to smack her across the face.

When she finished the second hamburger, she stared at him. When she asked the question she had probably been turning over in her head for quite some time, it was barely above a whisper. "Can I shower?"

"Would that make you feel better?"

She nodded but didn't make eye contact. His chest swelled with pride. *She's learning so quickly.* He just needed her to understand that he was in charge, the master, and she needed him. "Then, yes. I'll take you up into the house, but I need to know I can trust you. Are you planning on staying here with me?"

"Okay."

He stood quickly, grabbing the duct tape from the workbench, tearing off a strip with his teeth, and placing it back over her mouth. "I have to do this until I know I can trust you."

She nodded her understanding, keeping her eyes on the ground. *Submissive, the way she should be.* He walked her toward the hatch, gripping the back of her elbow. Before he lifted the steel door he pointed to the gun in his waistband.

"If you try to run, I'll kill you. If you look like you're going to run, I'll kill you. I don't want to, but you'll have left me no choice. Do you understand?"

He expected her eyes to be filled with tears, but instead, he was met with a determined gaze. She seemed resolute in her understanding, clear on the repercussions if she deviated from their understanding. Killing Teresa in front of her had the lasting impact he'd intended. She knew what he was capable of, and she knew he wouldn't be deterred. The risk of killing outside his usual plan was paying off, and his reward would be Jessica.

Chapter Eighteen

I'm just saying, maybe we should watch him for a bit before we go knocking on his door." Lucy had crossed her arms in the backseat and was staring out the window.

Erica gritted her teeth when she answered. "And I'm just saying, we need to see how he reacts to police officers showing up on his doorstep."

Diego turned the wheel, placing them on an old dirt road that led to the Wilds property. Although Jessica had broken up with Wilds a while ago, it was the only lead they had to follow up on. "Lucy, we know you've seen more cases than us, but we're actual cops. Please, just let us do our job."

Erica didn't bother to try to hide her smile. There wasn't an official game being played, but it was a tick in her win column all the same. When they pulled up to the old house, Erica and Diego spoke at the same time. "Stay in the car."

Erica didn't bother to look in the backseat; it wasn't necessary. She knew Lucy was rolling her eyes and probably mimicking their words.

The farmhouse had seen better days. One of the upstairs shutters was falling off the hinges, the old yellow paint was flaking off in strips, and the screen door had such a large tear that it wouldn't have kept any bugs from trespassing indoors. The old floorboards that made up the porch area creaked and whined when they stepped on them. A house that was probably a sight to see in its heyday was now nothing more than a shell of lost memories.

Erica hadn't been in school with any of the Wildses, who lived too far on the outskirts of town to go to the local school, but she had heard of them. They were known to be rowdy, loud-mouthed, and had no problems starting or jumping into fights. She had picked up Lance Wilds for public intoxication, twice. Mostly, though, they'd always kept to themselves and headed toward Melbourne for their real partying. At one time, there were about six of them in or around Clearbrook, but that number had dwindled over the years. She wasn't sure how many, if any, still remained.

Erica turned her back to the house and rolled up her sleeves, looking at Diego. The temperature had increased when the day shifted toward the afternoon. She could feel the sweat starting to slip down her back. "Do the Wildses still live here? I don't think I've seen any of them in years."

"I don't know, but someone is inside." He nodded toward the house. "Someone just peeked out the upstairs window."

"Man or woman?" she asked without turning around.

"Man."

Diego rapped on the door first. After a few moments of waiting, he knocked again, a little bit louder this time. "Clearbrook Police."

Erica walked to the side of the wide porch, trying to peer through the window. The curtains were drawn, all but a small opening. She saw someone moving around, but their back was turned. She instinctively put her hand on top of her weapon, unhooking the holster clasp with her thumb.

Diego pounded on the door, which opened before the fourth rap. The man who answered was wearing a stained white undershirt. His hair was greasy, disheveled, and graying. There was stubble on his chin, reaching up to his ears. But the most interesting thing about the disheveled man in front of her was the fact that she recognized him immediately. He was a bartender at Junior's. More accurately, he had been there the night before. He had been keeping a very close eye on the drunk woman Erica had followed to the bathroom. "Can I help you?"

Erica kept her hand on her weapon, but closed the clasp as Diego spoke. "We're looking for Lance Wilds. Is he around?"

The man scratched his face. "No, I'm his cousin, Frank."

"Does he live here?" Erica asked. The slight breeze, which had been the only relief from the warm air, seemed to disappear. It made the air heavy with midday heat, prickling her skin. The breeze also provided a brief and potent whiff of stale sweat from Frank's skin.

"He stays here sometimes, but he's away on a job right now. Rest of the family has moved on." Frank stepped outside, letting the old wooden door shut behind him. Erica was surprised the hinges didn't pop off when the door hit the frame. "Is he in trouble?"

"We just have some questions for him." Diego pushed his sunglasses up on his nose.

"About Jessica Vargas?"

"What do you know about Jessica?"

"I know she's missing, thanks to the stuff in the newspapers, and I know they used to date."

"Have you seen her?" Erica asked. She wasn't sure she'd believe his answer, regardless of what he said.

"Sure, from time to time. I work at Junior's, and she's there with her friends sometimes," he said. He was looking in their general direction but didn't make eye contact. He was looking past them, toward the car.

"Have you seen her lately?"

"Nah, not for a while." He pulled a cigarette pack from his back pocket, knocked one out of the top, stuck it in his mouth, then lit it.

"You said Lance was at a job. Where does he work?"

"He drives a truck. He does mostly long-haul jobs."

"What company does he work for?" Diego asked.

Frank wiped the sweat from his forehead with the back of his hand, taking a long breath. "No one in particular. He's an independent contractor. Companies don't like to pay out pensions anymore, so he gets more work that way."

"Where are Lance's parents? Can we speak with them?" Diego pushed.

"They live up in Oregon now. Couldn't take the summer heat anymore."

"What about Lance and Jessica, when was the last time you saw them together?" Erica asked.

He seemed to be thinking, but Erica got the impression he knew the answer. The smile that quickly appeared and then vanished immediately, spoke volumes. "It's been years. I couldn't say for sure."

Erica analyzed his body language. He was calm, almost bored with their conversation. *Something's off.* Most people would be asking questions, as many as they could think of, as quickly as possible. It wasn't often something like this happened in their small sleepy town, but it was as if this man couldn't be bothered.

Erica pulled her phone out and flipped to a picture of Claudia Ramos, and she turned it around to him. "Recognize her?"

He took a long drag of his cigarette, staring at Claudia. She watched his hands, and the left one seemed to twitch, but she couldn't be sure. "That's the dead girl. Claudia?"

Diego stood closer to him. "Did you know her?"

"No," he said without hesitation.

"You sure?" Erica put the phone back in her pocket.

He put the cigarette out in the ashtray, pushing the butt down over and over again. "Yeah, I'm sure. Look, I can tell Lance you stopped by, but if there's nothing else, I need to get ready for work."

Erica took a step backward and nodded toward the barn off to the side. "Mind if we take a look around?"

He smiled at her, and she expected to see yellowing teeth, but to her surprise, they were clean, gleaming white. She wondered if this was a side he kept hidden. A kept and cared about appearance, making it easier to approach women.

"Do you have a warrant?"

"No. Should we get one?" Diego challenged him.

"You can do whatever you want, but you aren't getting in without one." He stepped back inside. "Have a nice day, Officers."

They got back in the car and sat for a moment. Then Diego started the car and headed back down the dirt road. "What do you think?"

He was speaking to Erica, but Lucy answered. "I think you could've at least cracked a window in here. It's hot."

Erica ignored her and responded to Diego. "I'm not sure. He seemed a little too aloof and calm."

"Maybe you should've thrown him in the back of the hot car." Lucy pushed against Erica's seat to make her point.

"Yeah, I agree. Maybe we should get a warrant," Diego suggested.

"With what cause? We don't have anything to point to him. We could make a stretch with Lance being the ex and living here, but I'm not sure it's enough. We should follow him, though. Something about him just isn't right."

"I'm pretty sure I suggested that before we got here." Lucy's tone indicated she was growing irritated with being ignored.

"Tonight?"

"Yeah, I can do that," Erica said.

"I'm coming." Lucy leaned forward from the backseat.

"No, you aren't," they said in unison.

"Oh, suddenly you can hear me? And yes, I am. Look, I can help. I'm trained to notice things, pick up on cues, same as you. Plus, you both can't work twenty-four hours a day. I can go tonight with Erica. Diego can follow up tomorrow."

Neither Diego nor Erica said anything, knowing it wasn't a battle they were going to win. Lucy had already convinced the chief she was a valuable asset, and a stakeout wasn't altogether very dangerous. Lucy being in danger wasn't what concerned Erica at this moment. It was the thought of sitting in a car with her for hours on end, with nowhere to hide. Having to face those feelings and thoughts head on, with no viable escape plan, was intimidating.

❖

Lucy was practically tackled by Grayson and Holly when she got back to her parents' house. Scratches behind the ears appeased Holly, but Grayson wanted detailed information about every second they hadn't been together.

Twenty minutes later, the three of them were out by her parents' pool, drinking a beer and letting the late afternoon sun soak into their skin. Holly was stretched out on her own lounge chair, and Lucy smiled when she pictured her with a pair of sunglasses and a drink with a miniature umbrella resting inside.

"What's Sheila like?"

Lucy leaned back in her chair, her chin up toward the sun. "I wish I could say she was horrible, but she wasn't." She hadn't been sure what to expect, but it wasn't Sheila's kindness. It made Lucy feel guilty, having judged her before meeting her.

"Ugh, she was polite to you, even in the midst of her family tragedy? Awful."

"I know, right? I was hoping she'd be a total troll."

"So disappointing."

"Seriously."

"But you're going on this stakeout thing, tonight?"

"Yeah, but not just to spend time with Erica. It's good for the story too. It's not very often you get to tell a story directly from the cop's point of view. It's going to be a great scoop." It really would be a great aspect to the story, but she was trying to downplay her excitement about spending time with Erica. The idea of being with her, uninterrupted and alone, was exciting. Her chest squeezed with anticipation and nervousness. It was cliché, but she felt a bit like a teenager.

Her mom walked into the backyard, and once she was in their line of sight, she gently tapped the bottom of her hair.

Lucy smiled and took a swig out of her beer. "Hair looks nice, Mom."

"Oh, thank you. Grayson did it for me earlier."

He sat up, crossed his legs, and raised his beer bottle to her. "You look fantastic, Maria."

"Thanks to you, sweetie." She pointed at Lucy. "We're eating at your brother's for Erica's birthday. Lucy, change before we go. You aren't wearing that." She walked back inside.

Lucy looked down at her clothes. "How come she didn't tell you to change?"

"Because I exude gorgeous. It doesn't matter what I wear."

"At least it hasn't gone to your head."

"Oh, thank goodness. Could you imagine? God, that would be obnoxious."

Her mother's reference to changing her clothes was a bit annoying, but she wasn't wrong. She had been caught up in the thought of being able to spend time with Erica, and she hadn't actually wondered what that would mean. Nor had she considered what she wanted it to suggest. The thought of being with her without interruption was exciting, but to what end? Lucy suddenly felt overwhelmed. She had told herself over and over again that she needed to know one way or another if there was a prospect for them at all, even if it was only friendship. But that's not what her feelings were reflecting. Now she considered that what she wore could imply her intentions. *Jesus, this is more complicated than I remember.* But then again, she couldn't recall ever putting this much thought into any woman since Erica. That realization sat on her chest, constricting her breathing. *So much for looking forward to tonight.*

CHAPTER NINETEEN

Erica put the harness over Bella's body, which was always an exercise in patience. The short, lumpy hound fought her at every movement. Erica could never tell if it was out of excitement to go somewhere or stubbornness because she didn't want to leave her couch. It was probably a bit of both. Once it was finally on, Bella danced back and forth by the door, ready to leave.

Erica looked at her reflection one last time before leaving. She was going to be working immediately after dinner, so she needed to be dressed for both. She wore dark blue jeans and her favorite Iron Man T-shirt. "Do I look too much like a high school boy?"

Bella continued to stare at the door, ignoring any last-minute fashion decisions Erica was verbalizing. Erica shrugged. *Who am I trying to impress anyway? Lucy?* Yes was the obvious answer, but not the one she wanted. She attached her gun holster, put on her watch, and put her cell phone in her pocket.

It only took three minutes to get to Diego's house. If it were any other night she'd have walked over, but she needed to go to Junior's after, where Frank Wilds would be working. When she slowed her car in front of his house she took a moment to look through the large window that exposed his living room to the outside world. Having Lucy back created a bit of an alternate reality. A reality in which she had never left and things seemed to be as they should be. Other times, she could feel the distance and time that had separated them like a gash, a gash that had never fully healed. Any misstep, any movement, would make it pulse with pain.

She scratched the top of Bella's head. "You ready for this?" Bella yawned and scratched at the door, ready to get inside. "Okay, okay. Let's go."

Erica opened the door and Bella hopped out. She bent down to put her leash on, but Bella was already headed up the driveway and toward the front door. She was surprisingly fast for having such stumpy legs and paws the size of hockey pucks. Erica shook her head and followed behind.

By the time Erica reached the house, Bella had already been let inside and was turning circles in the living room with Holly.

"I think they like each other." Melanie, Diego's wife, hugged her.

"Bella isn't a hard sell." Erica squeezed her back, thankful that with so much uncertainty involving Lucy, Melanie and her family still remained a constant.

"Happy birthday, Chance." Melanie kissed her cheek.

"Thank you." She peeked inside. "It smells amazing in there."

Melanie stepped aside for Maria and Miguel to say their hellos. They hadn't gotten a word out when Erica felt an embrace at her knees. She leaned down and picked up the tiny human.

Sofia put her hands on either side of Erica's face and kissed her on the mouth. "Happy birffday, Aunt Erica."

Erica kissed her multiple times on both cheeks. "Thanks, bug."

She greeted everyone else, thanking them all for the birthday greetings. She finally made it over to the dining room table, where twenty different snacks were on display. She grabbed several tortilla chips and scoops of Melanie's homemade salsa. She felt Lucy come up behind her without having to look back. It was amazing that after all these years, she still knew when she was nearby. Even if she couldn't see her, her body knew.

"I can't believe you still have that stupid Iron Man shirt."

Erica wiped the salsa from the corner of her mouth. "It's not the same one. I had to replace my old one a few years back." She was careful to not let her gaze wander over to Lucy. She wasn't sure she could trust herself not to stare.

Lucy lifted her hand like she was going to touch the shirt but changed her mind. "And you went with the same design?"

"I like what I like. I try not to mess with that." She hadn't meant for there to be two meanings to her statement, but she realized there were when she saw Lucy's eyes get a bit sad.

Grayson bit down on a chip and pointed at the shirt in question. "I love it, so retro."

Erica laughed. "Yup, that's me."

Lucy put her hand on Erica's shoulder and pulled her closer so she could whisper in her ear. "Do you remember when you first bought that shirt?"

Erica knew she didn't mean the one she was wearing, but the original. She hadn't thought about it when she put it on this evening, but maybe, subconsciously she had. "Yes, I remember. You let us run out of gas."

Lucy tugged on the silver necklace that hung around her neck. It had been a sixteenth birthday present from Maria; she had loved it then, and it appeared, loved it still. "Is that the only thing you remember about that day?"

"No, it's not."

Lucy was close enough for Erica to see through the cotton weave of her red V-neck shirt. Red was Lucy's favorite color and it looked great on her. It always had. The color of love, fire, and passion. She quickly reminded herself it was also the color of stop, of warning.

Lucy grinned mischievously. "It didn't turn out so bad."

They'd run out of gas two miles outside of town. At the time, cell phones weren't commonplace, and they had to walk to the nearest gas station. They had only been about a mile into their walk when the skies opened up, and rain started coming down in droves. By the time they had gotten to the station, they were soaking wet and laughing.

Erica had taken the gas can and jogged back to the car to spare Lucy from having to go the two miles in the rain. By the time Erica picked her up, Lucy had purchased new shirts from the treasure trove of random clothing the gas station also had available. Lucy had already changed into a dry shirt, handing Erica an Iron Man shirt, a lucky find for a gas station hunt.

Erica hopped in the backseat as Lucy drove. She peeled off her pants to put on a pair of jeans she happened to have in her soccer bag from practice the day before. As she put the new shirt on, she could feel Lucy's eyes on her. The way she tracked her movements was exciting and a bit erotic. A few moments later, she pulled the car over and climbed into the backseat, removing the new shirt from her body...

Erica pulled herself away from the memory before it went any further and looked at Lucy. "It was a wonderful day. I think about it every time I smell rain."

She hadn't meant to say that last part and was embarrassed she had. She needed to step away from this conversation before she revealed anything else, not to Lucy, but to herself. "I'm going to see if your mom needs any help."

Erica walked away, and there was a blankness where moments before, Lucy had felt nothing but heat. She moved over to the couch and took a seat. She wasn't positive they had been sharing the same memory, but she hoped. Now she needed a bit of grounding and some time to observe everything she had been missing.

Lucy knew her family was close to Erica. It had been one of the reasons she stayed away, but she hadn't been prepared for the reality of it. Erica wasn't just close to her blood relatives, she was one of them, maybe even more so than her. They shared a plethora of inside jokes, glances, friendship, and love. Things Lucy had missed out on by following her career.

Her niece sat on Erica's lap in the kitchen, showing her several drawings she had made in kindergarten that week. Her parents spoke of her accomplishments as if she was their daughter, and Melanie handed her a cup of coffee without asking how she wanted it. Jealousy bubbled up inside her belly and worked its way through her body. But she couldn't decide if she was jealous of Erica, or of her family. The gravity of everything she had given up in both instances started to weigh on her, pushing on her shoulders, making it difficult to breathe.

Grayson took a seat next to her. "You okay?"

"I don't know."

"Which part are you upset about?"

She motioned to her family sitting only a few feet away. "I don't know what hurts more, that I could've been a part of this, or that they don't seem to miss that I'm not."

He rubbed her leg. "That's ridiculous. If you want to be a part of it, they'll welcome you back with open arms. They love you."

Her thoughts were interrupted by the front door hitting the wall behind it with a loud bang as it was flung open. Her brother MJ immediately followed the loud noise. The noise matched his personality. He hadn't aged a day, despite the year he had in age over Lucy. He was still as muscular as he had been when they were in their mid-twenties. His hair didn't have a single strand of gray, which Lucy figured was probably because of a coloring agent. His eyes were bright, his smile was wide, and as usual, his presence filled the whole room.

Grayson grabbed her arm, harder than what was necessary, and squeezed. "Who is that?"

"That," she sighed, "is MJ, my other brother."

"Oh my."

"Yeah, he gets that a lot."

Her mother practically fell over herself to get to him. She squeezed his cheeks and lavished them with kisses. "Oh my goodness, all my children together in one house again. What a wonderful day."

MJ picked her up and twirled her around in a large circle. He made his way through the rest of the family, giving hearty hugs and joyful pats on the back. He finally landed on Erica, and she stood to get his embrace.

"Chance! Man, you look great! I still can't believe my little sister ever gave you up."

Erica rubbed her hands down her pants, looking awkwardly toward Lucy on the couch. Lucy gave a halfhearted wave and MJ hurried over. He leaned over and swooped her up in his arms as if she weighed nothing at all.

"Lucy! Oh man, I didn't think you'd actually be here."

"I live to surprise you," she said flatly.

He put her down and put his hand out to Grayson. "Hi, I'm MJ."

Grayson smiled, extending his hand. "Grayson."

They locked eyes for what Lucy thought was a bit too long. Then he turned back around to his adoring fans. "Where is my newest niece? I came all the way from New York just for her."

Lucy sat back down on the couch, feeling dismissed.

"This is Gabriella, and she has been dying to meet you." Melanie walked over and handed him the squirming bundle in her arms.

"And here I thought Diego got all the looks in your family," Grayson said, fanning himself.

She patted his leg. "Sorry, buddy, you're not his type."

He raised a single eyebrow at her. "I'm everyone's type."

"Dinner!" Melanie called from the other room.

The amount of food displayed throughout the kitchen was mind-boggling. There were enchiladas, homemade tortillas, salsa, and taco fixings, even a few tamales. Grayson filled his plate and took a seat next to her again. "Do you think your family will adopt me?"

It was a rhetorical question, but it made her smile all the same. She was enjoying the togetherness, the laughter, and the simple happiness that was only accessible when she was with her family. However, it was short-lived.

"How's the local paper working out for you?" MJ asked between bites of food.

"Good."

"I still can't believe you turned down that job in DC."

MJ had been the only one she had told about the job offer. He worked for the same news station in DC, and she had sought out his advice before making her decision. She had finally opted against it because she wanted a slower pace after what had happened in the Middle East. She had also asked him to keep it between them, a tidbit he had either forgotten or was intentionally ignoring at this moment. She winced, not wanting to have this conversation with her family.

"What job?" her father asked.

"MJ, I thought you were bringing your girlfriend." She smiled at him incredulously.

"Change of plans."

"What's wrong with this one?" Her brother had a reputation of being a player, a very active player, for that matter.

He stared at her for a moment, his eyes pleading with her to be quiet. "It just didn't work out."

"Oh, I really liked Krissy." Her mom tried to throw an upbeat vibe to the jousting match.

"Her name was Kathy, and we just weren't right for each other."

Lucy laughed and shook her head.

"You're one to talk, Lucky."

"What's that supposed to mean?" She sat up straight, ready to play defense.

"The last time I saw you in DC you spent half the time crying into your wine about Erica." He pointed his fork at the object of her musing.

Lucy put her fork down and crossed her arms. "You're a special kind of dick, huh?"

Erica stood up, picking up her plate. "Melanie, dinner, as always, was amazing. Do you mind if I pack this up? Lucy and I have to be somewhere, for work."

"But you haven't had your cupcakes," her mom added.

"I know, and thank you. But we do have a missing woman and I really need to get back to work."

Lucy's mom looked disappointed but understood. Melanie stood up also and began to put items in a container. They both started saying their good-byes, and her parents assured Erica they would keep Bella for the night. Lucy said bye to everyone except MJ, and she made sure he realized it. The final look she shot him before walking out the door said it all.

Their competitive natures had always been part of their relationship. They goaded each other on, took shots at one another, but there were lines. Bringing up Erica, in *front* of Erica, was a clear and obvious line. She was embarrassed, not only by what he said, but that he had said it in front of everyone. MJ always told it to her straight, it was one of the reasons she went to him for advice, but that wasn't like him and she wondered what had gotten into him. She couldn't worry about that now though. The best course of action to try to regain any semblance of ease with Erica would be to do their jobs.

CHAPTER TWENTY

They pulled up outside the bar and Erica put the car in park. She had been nervous about this stakeout since its inception, but now there were different feelings whirling around inside her. Had Lucy really been thinking about her all these years, or was it just an alcohol-induced moment of weakness, brought about by a visit from a family member who knew them both? She was trying to think of what to say when Lucy saved her the trouble.

"What exactly are we waiting for?"

"I'm going to write down every license plate here tonight. We need to see who comes and goes, employees, customers, everyone. See if anything is out of place, or anyone acts strangely toward any women who are alone. Then, I want to follow Frank Wilds after his shift. I don't know how likely it is, but there's a possibility he may be in contact with Lance. I can't shake the feeling that he knows something." She busied herself by starting to jot down every license plate in the parking lot.

"I'm sorry for ruining your birthday party."

Erica continued to write, not bothering to look up. "You didn't ruin anything. It's no secret that you and MJ have always been crazy competitive."

"He just thinks he's better than everyone else. It's super annoying."

Erica laughed and shook her head. "Have you ever thought that he has his own stuff to deal with? You aren't the only one who struggles."

"What could he possibly be struggling with? His life is perfect." Lucy rested her arm next to the window, looking out.

"No one's life is perfect," she said without trying to give too much away. MJ had confided in her, and it wasn't her story to tell.

"Is he okay?" Her voice was filled with worry and sincerity. That was Lucy and MJ, they were each other's greatest competition, but as soon as there was a hint of trouble for either one, they would drop everything.

"Yeah, he's just dealing with some stuff."

"Stuff you can't tell me?"

If it had been twelve years ago, Erica would've told her what she knew. But it wasn't twelve years ago. It was now. It didn't matter how much she pretended or how long her stay was, as soon as this assignment was over, Lucy would be headed back to San Diego and she'd be left here. "It's not my stuff to tell."

Erica had expected an argument, a ploy to divulge what she knew, but it didn't come. Dark hair framed Lucy's face, the soft light from the parking lot falling across her lap. "Yeah, I get that." The look of understanding that traced over her features made her all the more beautiful.

"I wrote you a letter when I heard about what happened in the Middle East." Erica said it without thinking and wished she hadn't.

"I never got it."

"That's because I never sent it."

Lucy continued looking out the window. "I wanted to fly straight back here and see you after all that."

Erica was surprised by the sentiment. Lucy hadn't made a single attempt to talk to her in their years apart. She knew she had come home to visit a handful of times, but they had successfully avoided each other. "Why didn't you?"

Her answer came without hesitation. "You weren't mine to run home to anymore."

"I would've listened," she said sincerely.

Lucy looked contemplative. "I know, but that wouldn't have been fair to you."

There it was, the pang of reality. Lucy never wanted her back. She just wanted a familiar shoulder to cry on. "I understand."

"You know, when I got back, everyone kept telling me how brave I had been. Like it was some great act of heroism to keep the recorder on while we were under fire, while people died. That's not what it was at all." She took a deep breath, and there was a hitch in her voice as she fought back tears. "I kept recording, kept writing notes to use later, because I was too scared to do anything else. Everything was so out of control, I had to do something I knew how to do. That's all it was."

Erica remembered when the piece had come out. Ultimately, it had earned Lucy a Pulitzer Prize, but at the time, Erica could feel her fear with each written word. Her heart had hurt then for the best friend she had known, the girl she had once loved, and the woman a million miles away. But it had also been impactful, giving the people back home in the States a real picture of the terror the troops were dealing with. She had known it would have a lasting impact on Lucy. In fact, she worried often about which parts of her experience would change, harden, or altogether destroy the person she had known.

"Do you want to talk about it now?"

"It's a long story."

Erica chuckled. "We actually have a great deal of time on our hands."

Lucy chewed on her thumb. It was a nervous habit she'd had since she was a kid, apparently, one she had never managed to break. "I had been assigned to Operation Iraqi Freedom and had been over there as soon as I graduated college and got a job with the *San Diego Tribune*. I was mostly assisting the other reporters, trying to earn my stripes. I did a lot of legwork, research, and set up interviews, stuff like that. I was getting more bylines by the time Operation New Dawn went into effect in the late summer of

2010. We were covering the troop withdrawal from the area. We were on the move from Iraq to Kuwait, and it should've just been a normal day. We were doing feel-good stories, how the troops were feeling as they got closer to going home, what they missed, who they wanted to see, stuff like that. We had hopped out of the transport because we had a flat tire, no big deal. We were with the CNN team, who were taking B roll of the area. I was standing with the camera guy while he did his pan over the desert terrain. We saw it first. There was a man about a hundred yards away with a rocket launcher. I wanted to say something, I think I did say something, actually, but it was too late. He fired and it blew up one of the Humvees. We ran to take cover, and we managed to make it into one of the buildings, or something that used to be a building, there wasn't much left of it. But the shots kept coming, the loud bangs, the ground shook, and the wall we were hiding behind crumbled. It fell down on top of my friend, the camera guy from CNN. His camera was still working, so I set it up to record everything going on around us. I'd never been in front of the camera and I wasn't going to start then. I just wanted it documented so I could write about it later. People think I did it for a story, but I didn't. At the time, I did it because I wasn't sure what else to do, and also because I wanted some type of proof that we were there, that we were alive, that we weren't just dust."

Erica waited for her to continue. She wanted to reach out and touch her hand, to let her know she was there for her, but she didn't dare touch her. Lucy's mind was somewhere else right now, and Erica didn't want to startle her, or cause her undue stress.

"The troops that were with us, they called in our location, they fought off the insurgents, and they kept us safe. There was so much yelling, so much gunfire, and so much blood. The sky had gone black from all the dust, from the wall that had crumpled down around us. I don't know, maybe it wasn't actually black, but that's how it felt at the time. I could hear people in the distance. There were cries, yelling. But you couldn't tell from what side they were coming from. That was the weird part, ya know? All this devastation, death, horror, and you weren't sure who was suffering from it. That's the thing I remember most from being there. There was so much destruction, it was hard to tell who the victims were." She looked over at her now, and she forced a smile, but it didn't reach her eyes.

"Is that where the scar is from?" Erica asked.

Lucy rubbed her arm without looking down at it. "Yes, from the rebar."

"The rebar?"

"I tried to pull out Bruce, the camera guy, when I heard him whimpering. I don't remember how long I spent trying to pull the pieces of the wall off him. I remember being so incredibly tired. At one point, I slipped and came down on a piece of rebar that was sticking out of the wall that had fallen on top of him. I was lucky it didn't go through any major veins, or I wouldn't be here today. When I replay it in my head, I'm sure he was trying to cry out, but he couldn't force more than a whimper. I wasn't strong enough though, no matter what I did, and his cries just got quieter and quieter. Then, after a while, he didn't make any noise at all. He was just quiet, that scary kind of quiet. The kind of quiet that only comes after death."

"I'm so sorry, Lucy." It didn't feel like enough. She wanted to give her more, but she didn't have the words.

Lucy blinked several times before seeming to come back to this plane of existence. "It's okay. But I think my therapist took her last trip to Bora Bora on my fees alone."

Erica wanted to tell her that she could've come to her, that she'd have been there for her. But was that the truth? If Lucy had come knocking on her door all those years later, would she have answered? Erica silently told herself she would've, but she wasn't sure if she was just lying to herself because of Lucy's story.

Lucy broke her internal reflection. "I never should've left you all those years ago. It's one of my biggest regrets." Her voice was barely a whisper, but the words seemed to echo, loud and clear.

Erica felt like she'd been sucker-punched. She had spent months, years, wanting to hear those exact words, but they'd never come. And now, twelve years later, as they sat in a parking lot on some weird cop and reporter stakeout, which would never fly in a big city, Lucy bared her soul. Erica's emotions were all over the place, caught between empathy for what Lucy had told her and anger for what Lucy had done to her.

"That's not fair."

"I know," Lucy said immediately, apparently prepared for the answer. "I should've told you years ago. I shouldn't have let all this time pass. I should've come home to you."

Erica felt the brush of her hand on top of hers. "But you didn't." Erica pulled her hand away. "That night, after you told me we had to end our relationship, I drove home feeling like I had a knife in my heart. No, worse than that, you ripped out my heart. You didn't just break up with me, Lucy, you ended our friendship, too. All those years, all those promises, all those memories. You just walked away."

"I didn't want it to be that way. I wanted to give you space. Actually, maybe I needed to give myself space. I thought being with you was holding me back, which I realize now was ridiculous. I thought I wasn't having the full college experience because I was involved with someone. Plus, everyone around me had broken up with their high school sweethearts and were playing the field. I thought I should do the same, like I was missing out on something."

"Were you? Did you find what you were looking for?"

Lucy rubbed her palm with her thumb and stared at the floor of the car. "No. All I figured out was how much I missed you, how much I needed you. So I ran. I tried to escape from my problems, and I've been running every day since."

"You expect me to believe you missed me so much that you never contacted me? That it was so hard for you to be away that you never texted? Please, I'm not that stupid." Erica was fighting down a whirlwind of emotions. They were bouncing around in her head, tiny jumping beans she couldn't get under control. Each one tapped a different emotion—confusion, anger, and betrayal.

"I was scared that you would've turned me away. And whenever I thought about doing it anyway, it always felt like the wrong time."

"And what if that's how I feel now?" She watched Lucy closely, wanting to see if her reactions would mimic her words. She needed to know if this was genuine or if she was simply trying to clear her conscience.

"I'm sorry I hurt you, Erica. You're the last person I ever wanted to cause pain. I know you might not believe that, but it's true." She took a deep breath but didn't look up.

"You're unbelievable. You show up here, after years have passed. You insert yourself into our investigation, spend maybe a total of twelve hours with me, and decide you want to be part of my life again. I'm not the same person I was when that car pulled away twelve years ago. You don't even know me anymore."

"I've never stopped thinking about you."

"That's not good enough, Lucy. You could've had this conversation with me at any point in the last decade. Why should I believe you now?"

"Because it's the truth; it's always been the truth."

"And the other side of the truth is what I went through. You still have no idea how difficult losing you was for me."

"Maybe you don't know me anymore, either. I've been through things that forced me to reevaluate my choices, the things I've done."

"Maybe not, but I'm not chasing a ghost. You're trying to fix something that can never be repaired. You broke something in me that night. More than my heart, you broke my trust. I've spent years and countless relationships trying to get it back, but it will never be the same. I don't think it's supposed to be. And now I'm just supposed to put it all in the past and be your what? You haven't even told me what you want."

"That's because I don't know what I want. I thought I wanted closure. I thought I wanted to put this to rest, to let you go once and for all. Now, I'm not sure what—"

Lucy was still talking, but Erica had zeroed in on the figure walking out of the building.

"It's Frank Wilds." She tapped Lucy and pointed across the parking lot. Erica started the car. "Time to see where this guy goes at night."

His car made a right out of the parking lot, and Erica followed. She managed to put a car between them for the time being, but that wouldn't hold. This was a small town and if he was going to eventually make it to the back roads, it would be clear someone was following him. The car in front of her made a left, and she fell back a bit farther when her phone rang.

She glanced at the caller ID and answered. "Detective Chance."

She heard the words on the other end but couldn't quite wrap her head around them. She slowed the car and checked the rearview mirror, then made a U-turn.

Lucy looked over at her. "What's up?"

Erica tossed the phone back down in the cup holder. "There's another body."

CHAPTER TWENTY-ONE

Lucy stared out the window, watching the flashes of the police lights beat against the empty fields. In a few months, they would be spilling over with corn, something Lucy hadn't seen in years. She tried to focus on the eerie familiarity of her childhood and ignore the feelings that buzzed through her from the conversation she had with Erica. She wasn't sure what had come over her in that moment. She hadn't said anything she didn't mean, but she had wanted to time it better. She wanted to have a relationship with Erica; she just wasn't sure what that meant. But above all, she wanted her to know how sorry she was, how sorry she remained. Instead, she let it dribble out, unable to stop once it started. It was like she had picked a scab which, once open, wouldn't stop bleeding.

She was mercifully rescued from her internal reflection and thrust into another person's far worse tragedy when they turned down Orwood Road. She recognized Diego's car as they slid up behind it. He was already having uniformed officers tape off a perimeter as they got out of the car.

His expression was tired, pained by yet another small-town travesty. "It's not Jessica Vargas."

Erica's eyes flashed a look of relief and then anger when she looked past him to the body on the ground. She put her hands on her hips and kicked the dirt. "Damn it."

He nodded toward the two teenagers who were wrapped in a blanket and sitting on a log. "They found her, but we don't have a lot of other information."

Erica pushed past him and went to look at the body. Lucy didn't bother to follow, knowing full well she needed to stay out of the crime scene area. She stood next to her brother, who was making notes in his notebook.

"Does it look like the same guy?" she asked.

Diego looked at her briefly and then continued to write. "Everything is the same except for the fact that she wasn't from around here. Also, her car was parked about fifteen feet away. Her driver's license says she's from Salinas, and we couldn't find anything that would point to why she'd be here in Clearbrook."

"How do you know she isn't affiliated with Clearbrook?" Lucy asked.

"Well, I guess we can't be sure yet, but she hasn't been reported missing to us, and we're checking with the Salinas Police Department."

"Same age?" Lucy asked.

"Just about. Teresa is twenty-five."

"Jesus Christ." She felt goose bumps prickle up her skin.

"Any luck with Frank Wilds?"

"We were following him when we got the call." *And saying things that should have been said long ago.*

"Where was he headed?"

Lucy shrugged. "Can't say for sure, but it was the right route to go back to his house."

"Damn."

"I'm going to contact the *Clearbrook Press* and see if they'll let me write a story, an update of sorts. You never know; it could shake something loose."

"Or it could enrage him."

Diego was right. Writing the story was a fifty-fifty shot. "Yeah, but if you two are right and this is the same killer from twenty-five years ago, I bet he's pissed that he hasn't gotten the recognition he probably thinks he deserves." It had been her experience that on some level, these mad men wanted recognition for their work. Even if he didn't realize it, he would once he saw his name in print.

He seemed to consider it for a moment. "We'll have to check with the chief."

"Yeah."

"She won't like the idea." He nodded in Erica's direction, who was still kneeling next to the body. She was jotting in her notebook and looking around the body, probably for any clue she could find. Erica would think Lucy was putting herself in danger, and she would think an article with her name on it was too dangerous.

"No, probably not."

"I'll make the call." He sighed.

Two hours later, Lucy was sitting in front of her computer screen. She watched the cursor blink at her from the blank page, mocking her. The kitchen table was littered with several files she had been given permission to make copies of for the story. Holly and Bella lay at her feet, curled in a joined ball of snores and blissful ignorance. Erica had dropped her off at her parents' house to write the story while she went back to the office. As she had suspected, she didn't like the idea of giving this monster any kind of recognition, but the chief had groggily agreed when Diego made the phone call.

Grayson came downstairs and poured himself a glass of water, taking a seat at the table next to her. "What's all this?"

She continued to stare at her computer screen, waiting for the words to magically start appearing before her eyes. The tone and sentiment of this article could mean the difference in that fifty-fifty split, and the implications were stressful. She was accustomed to stress from her job, but not of this nature. This story could mean the difference between life and death for Jessica Vargas.

She touched his hand. "You should go home. I don't know how long I'll be up here. I know you don't like flying, but there's a train that runs from Stockton to San Diego."

He drew a few circles on the table with his finger. "I think I'm going to stay up here for a bit. Clearbrook is kind of growing on me, and I've got a ton of vacation time."

She looked up from her computer, suspicious. "What?"

"I like your family, and this little town has a lot of charm."

"Charm?"

He rolled his eyes. "Am I cramping your style or something?"

"No, I just thought you'd want to get out of here as soon as possible. What was it you said? You hoped the horse smell didn't stick to your clothes?"

"I didn't say that."

"Yes, you did."

"Well, whatever, I changed my mind. You get used to the horse smell. Besides, I'm going to go visit Napa."

"With who?"

"I know people."

"You know exactly eight people here, and that includes me."

"When did you become so nosy? I'm going with your parents and MJ."

"MJ?" Lucy hoped she was able to hide her bitter tone and mask it as curiosity instead. Was everyone in her family eager to spend time with everyone but her?

"Yeah, you know that guy you're related to?"

"I just don't understand—"

He cut her off before she was able to finish her thought. "What is all this anyway?"

She decided to let the subject drop, at least for now. Her underlying family issues had been in place for years and wouldn't be solved in one conversation with Grayson. "I'm going to write a story, try to draw this guy out."

He leaned back in his seat. "Are you sure that's a good idea?"

"I need to do something. People are dying and there's a woman still missing."

"And you're a reporter. Maybe you should let the police handle this."

"I am. I'm helping. You know, where I can. The way I do things."

He was quiet for a long moment, clearly turning something over in his head. "You know, putting yourself in danger won't bring Erica back to you."

"Good to know you have such a high opinion of me. I'm doing this because it's my job, people have a right to know, and because it could help."

"It could also make you a target."

"That's ridiculous."

"Is it? Have you looked at these women? You share some similarities."

"Yes, a few, but they're much younger than me." She had noticed a pattern with all of the women. She knew what they shared regarding looks, upbringing, and ethnicity. But it wasn't enough to scare her off the story, or from trying to help. She survived the Middle East. She could take care of herself.

"Oh? And how do you know he won't make an exception if you piss him off?"

"Grayson, I'm a reporter. This is what I do, and I'm going to do it. I don't need your approval or permission."

He put his hands up in surrender. "Okay. No need to get all 'I am woman, hear me roar.'"

"You're supposedly a feminist," she practically shouted.

"Sure! Equal pay, pro-choice, down with the pussy grabbing president, rah-rah-rah! But I can set all that aside when it puts my best friend in danger."

"I'll be fine." It was a mantra she had repeated to herself over and over again in a variety of situations. Sure, it lacked eloquence, but it had worked in the past and it would work now.

He stood and kissed the top of her head before heading back upstairs. "I hope you're right."

After she heard the bedroom door close she went back to the cursor on her screen, still blinking with nothing in its wake. She took a long sip of the Pinot Noir that sat next to the files on the table. She flipped one open and started turning through the pages. At the moment, her life was far from perfect. By her own hand, she had kicked up ancient dust, leaving her in a cloud of confusion and jumbled feelings. But writing a story was something she was good at and comfortable doing. She could help these women, Clearbrook, and maybe regain her footing emotionally. *When all else fails, write.*

"Talk to me, ladies."

Chapter Twenty-two

His left hand twitched as he flipped over the front page of the *Clearbrook Press*. They had released a special edition, just for him. Anger and pride surged through his body in equal measure. He wanted to tear Lucy Rodriguez limb from limb for exposing, in detail, the happenings of his conquests. This would inevitably cause panic and fear in the community, making his job that much harder. On the other hand, seeing it all laid out in black-and-white was a monumental accomplishment.

He read about each of the victims, feeling the saliva build in his mouth as he relived each kill like it was happening all over again. The part she missed was how it had been their own doing each time. Sure, he may have doled out the deathblow, but that was only because each of these women refused to give him what he wanted, what he deserved. Angelica Peña and Mariana Cruz had been so long ago, a lifetime to some. But now he could remember the way their hair had felt beneath his fingertips, the sound of their screams, and the way their eyes changed as the life drained out of them.

He walked up the stairs to his bedroom and pulled the vent grate off the wall. Behind it sat a small wooden box that contained the only material memories he had of the women, eight earrings. He picked each up, examining the small pieces of jewelry, holding them in his hands. It was the only thing he had left of them, the only way he could be close. They might not have lived up to his expectations, but they had been special all the same. In a separate box was the earring of Teresa Ortiz. She might not have taken up a space within his soul the way the others did, but she was special too. But her earring didn't deserve to be in his cherished box. He hadn't spent time with her; he had never wanted her. He simply needed her, as both a warning to Jessica and a way to throw the police off course a bit. No, her memory wouldn't share space with the others.

Teresa had been the first he hadn't gotten to know intimately. Taking her had been impulsive, exciting, and without any purpose besides buying him time with Jessica. For that reason alone, she could prove to be the most significant of any of them. He spoke to the earring as if it were tied to the soul of the owner. "Your death won't be in vain, dear girl."

He dropped the items into the different boxes and headed back downstairs. He had a few hours before his next shift, and he wanted to spend them with Jessica. He wanted to bring her the newspaper, show her everything he had accomplished, everything he had done, just to find her. Then she'd see just how special she was to him.

He grabbed several pieces of bread, some jam, and a banana. He tucked the newspaper under his arm and headed out to the barn. Once inside, he lifted the large steel door that led underground, turning on the light before he walked down the steps.

Jessica was huddled on the small, makeshift bed he had made her. Her eyes were rimmed with red and the dark smudges under them were more prominent than the day before. He was glad he had let her shower. The blood from Teresa Ortiz no longer colored the side of her face.

She slid off the bed and sat kneeling, head down, as he approached. *She's learned so well.* He spread jam on the bread, put the banana next to it, and put the plate in front of her. "Eat."

She hesitated for only a moment before putting the food in her mouth. "Thank you," she murmured between bites.

He tossed the newspaper in front of her. "I brought you some reading material too."

She scanned the pages, various levels of disgust and fear dancing across her expression. The more she read, the more infuriated he felt. "Don't you see, none of them mattered until you?"

She said nothing. She simply folded up the paper and sat back against the wall.

"They weren't grateful for what I'd done. I saved them from themselves, from their existences. They were wasting their lives, and I tried to help them."

"Is that really what you think you're doing?" As soon as she said it, she covered her mouth and lowered her head.

He strode across the room, kicked the plate out of the way, and knelt in front of her. He grabbed her shoulders, forcing her to look up at him. "They weren't worthy."

She let out a quiet sob, her body limp in his hands. "What did they do that was so wrong?"

He threw her backward, taking small satisfaction when her head hit the wall. "They were liars."

"Liars?"

He walked over to his workbench and pulled a knife off the wall. He returned, put it against her cheek, and waited for her tears to coat the blade. "I asked Angelica out on several occasions. She turned me down each time, telling me she had a boyfriend. Then, one night, I saw her go home with a man she had met that night. She lied to me, humiliated me, and probably laughed with her friends about it." He gently slid the blade down her cheek, leaving a small, wet, red line in its wake. "Mariana let me buy her two drinks and then turned me down. Again, a liar and a cock tease. There have been more over the years. Women who didn't or wouldn't see my worth. Women I had high hopes for, who turned out to be just as disappointing as the first few. They thought they were smarter than me, better than me, but I fixed that. I helped them to see just how powerful I was." He looked down at her, willing her to see what he was really saying. "I'm not a monster. I made them presentable, almost beautiful. I cleaned them up and even scrubbed their nails.

They didn't deserve it after the way they'd treated me, but I did it for them anyway."

She turned her head for the first time and looked him in the eyes. "You killed them because they didn't want to sleep with you?"

He pulled the blade from her face and licked the blood from the edge. "I gave them a chance to change their minds, so it's their own fault. They put themselves on display for the world. They were begging men to take what they wanted. Then, when one finally took them up on their offer, they acted surprised and scared. I took my time with each one of them, allowing them the opportunity to see things my way. But you're a stubborn group. Women believe they can behave however they wish with no repercussions. Turns out, I was their repercussion. I proved that point with each blow of the hammer. I've had to go through so many to get to you."

"What about me?" she asked softly, her voice shaking. "What did I ever do to you?"

He rubbed his face against hers, smudging the blood away with his own skin. "You're different. I could tell the first time I saw you that you weren't like the others. Claudia, she let men buy her drinks, night after night, and then would just go home with her friends. You, though, you're pure."

"Pure?"

He kissed her forehead and held her tightly as she tried to pull herself away. "You're mine. I knew it the first time I saw you."

"How long have you been watching me?"

"The first time I saw you cry, in the parking lot of Junior's, I knew I wanted you with me forever. It hadn't mattered that you were with my cousin. I knew he was no good for you, that he would fuck it up, and he did. He was never good enough for you. No one is. Just me."

She grew still against him. He waited for the tremor of fear to vibrate through her body and felt all-powerful when it finally materialized. "I'm going to prove how much you mean to me. I'm going to bring you a present. Then you'll see."

CHAPTER TWENTY-THREE

Erica watched as Jessica's boyfriend, Zack, buried his head in his hands. They had been questioning him for the last forty-five minutes, and either he was the world's best liar, or he really had no idea where Jessica was. She knew somewhere deep down it was the latter.

"You're free to go. Just stay close by."

He wiped the tears from his eyes with the back of his hand. "I'm not leaving Clearbrook without Jessica."

He was telling the truth. His feelings for Jessica were written all over his face and in his body language. The irony didn't escape her that she wouldn't have recognized that without having loved Lucy the way she had.

Initially, she hadn't liked the idea of Lucy writing a piece on the investigation, but she had to admit, it turned out better than she had hoped. It was an excellent tribute to the women who had lost their lives at the hands of a psychopath. It also served as a warning to the public to stay aware of their surroundings. Lucy was talented, she always had been, and if anything, she had only gotten better over the years.

She walked out of the conference room and sat at the large table, staring again at the four women whose pictures hung in contrast to the stark white of the board. Erica believed the person responsible had taken more lives. He wouldn't have just stopped after the first two kills were so close together. He had to have moved on, probably to a different state, making it difficult to track. At any given time, there were anywhere from twenty-five to fifty active serial killers, just in the United States. Unsolved murders went unrecognized when the killer remained a step ahead. They left little to no evidence and then moved on to the next town, the next victim. If databases didn't talk to one another, or if they failed to make connections for other reasons, there was no way to connect interstate murders. But something had brought this guy back to Clearbrook. The victims' deaths spanned over two decades, and they had too much in common, regardless of the years that separated them. Their hairstyles were different, their clothing, their means of communication, their places in the world. But there was still a string of similarities that didn't stop at their ethnicity. They had the world at their fingertips. Their stories were just beginning, prior to being tragically cut short by a madman. One of the unknown variables was to what extent the world would suffer because they were no longer in it. Each of them could have been a key to something different. One could have held the cure for cancer in her head, another could have been the love of someone's life, changing them forever. They each had something to offer that would be left untapped, undiscovered. Their deaths weren't just sad, they were absolute tragedies.

Then there was Jessica. She fit somewhere in this mix as well. She was the only one they could save from the fate the others weren't fortunate enough to avoid. *Maybe. If she's not already dead.* She looked at the list of items sent for processing from Teresa's car. There wasn't much to go on, just like Jessica's. Her car had been wiped clean except for a partial print. It was a small, tiny possibility that left her feeling anxious and excited.

There were items scattered across the table sealed in evidence bags. She picked up the bag that held Teresa's graduation tassel. Class of 2010. It must have held significance beyond the simple fact of graduating to still be hanging on her rearview mirror seven years later. She let her fingers feel the threads through the plastic, hoping it would send her a hint or a clue to anything that might have happened to the woman who had placed it where she could see it every day.

"Detective Chance?"

Erica swiveled in her seat. "Yeah?"

"There's a Francisco Cruz here to see you."

She mentally flipped through acquaintances in her head until she fell on the association. Francisco Cruz was the father of Mariana Cruz, one of the victims from twenty-five years ago. "Send him in."

Francisco Cruz was probably a very striking man when he was younger. His face wore the signs of a lifetime of pain, which probably started the day his daughter was taken from him. "Mr. Cruz," she said as he took the seat she offered. "What can I help you with?"

He carried a small notebook against his chest. "I saw the story in the paper today."

"I'm sorry. That must have been difficult for you."

His mouth formed a tight line. "No, Detective, what has been difficult is having spent the last twenty-five years without this man being caught."

There was no appropriate response. He was right, and placating him would do no good. "I can't imagine. What can I help you with?"

"I want you to look at my daughter's journal. Back then, they looked through it but said there was nothing in there. I want you to look at it now."

She took the notebook that he slid across the desk. "They looked at this?"

"Yes, but I thought maybe, with you looking at new cases, there might be something new, something they didn't see before. There has to be *something*. Mariana was a good girl, and she didn't deserve what happened to her. I know none of them did, but she… she was my baby." His voice hitched and he fought back tears.

"We're going to do everything we can."

"That's what they said back then, too." His hands formed tight balls in his lap. "Losing Mariana was the worst thing that ever happened to my wife and me. My wife passed about ten years ago, but she was gone long before that. Died of a broken heart the day they found Mariana's body."

"I can't imagine." She meant every short syllable.

He stared at her; she assumed to assess whether she was up for the task at hand. "I knew your grandpa. He was a good man, and I was sorry to hear of him passing. You look just like him. Funny how that happens, huh, the things that get passed on?"

She wanted to ask him more about her grandfather, but this wasn't her moment. It belonged to him and the memory of his daughter that was etched in his sad eyes.

He reached across the desk and put his hand back on top of the notebook. "They're never really gone, those who leave us. I think love is the only thing stronger than the pull of death. If you can still feel that love burning somewhere in your soul, then you never have to say good-bye."

She felt his simple and profound words penetrate the carefully constructed defenses she'd erected whenever she handled matters of the heart, whether they were hers or someone else's. "Thank you for the journal."

He stood to leave. "I hope it helps. I couldn't do anything to help Mariana, but I hope her words, even all these years later, help to protect someone else."

Once he had left, she started flipping through the pages of the journal. It was interesting to see the thoughts of a young woman from nineteen ninety-two, a time before a generation had learned to place every thought and emotion in a public forum on social media, for everyone to read.

She skimmed page after page, jotting down names, places, dates, anything. It wasn't until she got halfway through that she saw a familiar name. *Frank Wilds.* Frank apparently had a bit of an unhealthy obsession with Mariana.

Frank Wilds bought me another drink at Junior's tonight. I told him before I wasn't interested, but he insisted and said it was rude to refuse. I was trying to be polite, so I accepted. Then when Jill and I went to leave, he was hanging out by our car. He offered to drive us home, and when we refused he kicked the tire. So weird.

She flipped a few more pages and found him mentioned again. Her heart pounded at the possibility this journal was creating. It was their first real lead and they desperately needed it.

I don't know what it's going to take. Frank can't seem to take a hint. He invited me and my friends back to his place. Obviously, we weren't going to go with him. Who does that? We even told him we have boyfriends, which we totally don't, but figured he would get the hint. I was the DD tonight, and when I ordered a Diet Coke, he spit in it before he handed it to me. Jill said I should tell the manager, but we go there too often. I didn't want more issues in the future. What a weirdo.

But it wasn't until she turned to the final page of the journal she knew she had him.

Okay, seriously, what is Frank's problem? He followed me to the bathroom tonight and tried to force his way into the girls' room! Um, what's his damage? I ran out and grabbed Jill. We're never going back there. Ew, as if.

Erica tried to tamp down her anger and frustration. She reminded herself that sexual assault wasn't as widely talked about twenty-five years ago as it was today. Mariana wouldn't have realized this was a reportable offense, and she wouldn't have known where to turn except her girlfriends. But even if that were true, the officers who read this back then should've at least questioned Frank, just based on this journal alone.

She picked up the notebook and headed downstairs to the small call center in the basement of the building. She took deep breaths on the way down, wanting to keep an open mind. Just as she had hoped, Robbie Kern was sitting at the desk with a headset on, waiting for another call.

"Can I talk to you for a minute?"

"Sure," he said and buzzed her through the door.

She flipped the journal open to the first entry that mentioned Frank Wilds and put it in front of him. "I've looked through the notes, and you guys didn't even interview him. Why?"

He read the entry carefully. Then he flipped through a few more pages, continuing to read. He put the book down and rubbed his chin. "We wanted to, but we couldn't find him."

"Couldn't find him?"

"Yeah, his aunt said he had gone back up to Reno."

Erica gripped the desk she was leaning against. She didn't need to look down to know her knuckles were white. "You didn't put out an APB? No one thought to go up there and bring him back for questioning?"

Robbie looked down, shaking his head. "You have to remember, Chance, we were a really small department back then. There were only eleven of us on the entire force. Things weren't all fancy the way they are now."

"You could've called up to Reno PD."

"I did, and they said they'd look for him and let us know if they found anything. But they said they didn't have any sign of him there, and the only evidence we had were these entries. We didn't have anything solid."

"Kern, we have four dead women and another one is missing." She did her best to bite down on her rage, but she knew it wasn't all that convincing; her words had an edge and he clearly felt it.

His face flushed red. "You don't think I know that, Chance? Those women have haunted me every day of my life. That's why I came to you in the first place, remember?"

She didn't want to hear any more, or rather, couldn't hear any more. "You had enough for a warrant. You could've searched that house."

"We *did* search the house. We didn't find anything," he said, not making eye contact.

"Did you talk to Angelica's parents? Maybe she kept a journal."

"Yes, we asked. She didn't keep one. It wasn't like it is today, where every teenage girl writes every thought and feeling on social media."

"Did you ask them about Frank Wilds? Did she ever mention him?"

He rubbed his temples because he was either tired or felt guilty. She unfairly hoped it was guilt. "They never mentioned him. And I personally talked to the parents on several occasions."

She crossed her arms, staring down at him in his chair. "Is there anything else that could help get me a warrant? Anything at all?"

"If there was, I would tell you. I agree he's a damn good suspect, just like he was back then. It's no coincidence he's back and there are more dead women. We couldn't nail the bastard back then. Maybe you can this time."

She headed back upstairs without responding. Diego and Lucy were there waiting when she returned. She slid the journal over to the two of them and picked up the phone. "Take a look. I'm going to see if I can get a warrant for Frank Wilds's property."

CHAPTER TWENTY-FOUR

Lucy watched as Erica read the journal entries to a judge over the phone. A few moments later, she ended the call and threw her phone down. "God dammit."

"Did he tell you that you need more current evidence to search the home?"

Erica shot her a cold look. "I forgot you were such an expert. It was worth a try. I know that piece of shit did it. I know he has her. Like Kern said, it's no coincidence."

"Let's go get more evidence then," Diego said, standing up. "It damn well doesn't hurt to check the place out and see if he's there."

Erica's eyes lit up and she headed out the door, ready to go.

Lucy touched her brother's arm. "I'm going to sit this one out."

He looked at her, confused. "You sure?"

"Yeah, I have a few other places I want to dig around."

He shrugged and was gone without giving her a second glance.

Lucy walked out of the police station and started down the familiar streets. Some shops had come and gone, but their façades remained the same. The theater which offered two-dollar movies on Tuesday nights still had its old town charm, its sign looking like the last remnant from the nineteen fifties. Bakeries, hair salons, and a few new places bustled with midmorning patrons.

After a few blocks, she reached the Starbucks she had been seeking. She went inside and pretended to study the menu, even though she could recite her typical order without hesitation. She took a look around at the employees and was caught off guard to see Sheila at the barista bar. She ordered her drink and waited patiently, scanning the community board and making every effort not to make eye contact with Sheila.

Lucy grabbed her cup when her name was called and headed outside to the small green tables. A few moments later, Sheila approached her.

She smelled the coffee on her clothes and thought maybe if this reporting thing didn't work out, she wouldn't mind smelling like Starbucks.

"Lucy?"

"Sheila, hi."

"Mind if I sit?"

Lucy motioned to the empty seat in front of her. *If we can form some type of relationship, I might be able to get her to do an interview later.* "Please, be my guest." *Be professional. Don't focus on the fact that she's Chance's girlfriend. Focus on the story.*

"It's my first day back, but I'm having a difficult time concentrating. I thought it would be good for me to work, but now I'm not so sure."

"Have you worked here long?" She was fine with small talk and hoped she could keep it on track.

"Um, yeah. Since I was about eighteen, I guess. I became a manager about ten years ago."

"Cool!" *Cool? Maybe small talk isn't your thing.*

She managed a smile, but it didn't reach her eyes. "I just wanted to clear the air."

"About what?"

"About Erica."

Jesus, was she such a horrible person that she made this poor woman feel obligated to come have a ridiculous conversation in the midst of a family crisis? Some real self-reflection was going to be required after this. "About Chance? Sheila, you don't have to. I can't imagine what you're going through. Chance and I were a long time ago. There's no need to say anything."

"All the same, I'd like to anyway."

"Okay."

But now that she had the opportunity, Sheila seemed like she wasn't sure she wanted to say anything at all. She looked down at her hands. "She's very special."

"Yes, she is."

"No, I mean…yes, she is special, but I didn't mean it like that. I know Erica's rules. Four months is her limit and that's where we are. I know how she feels about me."

"Yes, it seems like you're very important to her." The words burned like acid leaving her lips.

"Thank you, but that's not what I meant. Erica's never going to love me. We have no future together, and I have no misconceptions about that. I've known that since the day we started dating. Hell, everyone kind of knows that."

"Sheila, maybe this is a conversation you should be having with Erica." She was curious as to where this was heading, but she also didn't want to get involved in Erica's relationships.

"No, you're the only person I can have it with. Erica is never going to love me or anyone else, because Erica will always love you."

The words hurt because she knew they weren't true. Maybe at one time, but not anymore. "No, trust me, that ship has sailed."

"Has it for you?" The look on her face indicated she knew she was being forward, but she didn't seem to care. "Look, maybe it isn't my place, but when your family goes missing, you tend to reevaluate. That, and I'm pretty sure you get a pass on social couth."

Lucy was caught off guard by her questions, but she could appreciate how an event in someone's life would impact their outlook. She didn't owe her an answer, but she wanted to give her the truth. It was the least she could do for her. "Honestly, I'm not sure."

The answer made Sheila smile. "Well, don't stop trying. She's worth it."

"I know she is."

Sheila got up to leave. "Sorry to bother you."

"It was no bother." She paused for a moment. "You're worth it too, you know."

That made her smile, too. "Yeah, I do."

Sheila was almost back inside when Lucy looked around the patio and noticed the cameras aimed at the door. "Sheila?"

"Yeah?"

"Were you working the night Claudia Ramos went missing?"

Sheila rubbed her arms, probably to push away the question that hit a little too close to home. "No, I wasn't. But Erica and Diego already checked the cameras and no one followed her out of the store."

"What about before she came in?"

"I don't know."

"Do you mind?" Lucy pointed to the store. It was unlikely she'd see anything they'd missed, but double-checking never hurt. They hadn't known who they were looking for before. Now they knew Frank Wilds was a likely suspect.

"Of course not. Come on back."

Sheila sat at the computer station in the small office and pulled up files with different dates. She found the one they were searching for and opened it.

"We should look at the two hours prior to Claudia coming in." Lucy hovered behind Sheila's chair. Her body hummed with the possibility of finding Frank Wilds lurking around the coffee shop.

"Do you know who you're looking for?"

Lucy suddenly had a pang of conscience. She shouldn't be looking at this with Sheila. They assumed the same man who took her cousin had also killed Claudia. She thought for a moment about walking out and saying she needed to get Erica.

Sheila must have sensed her hesitation because she turned and made eye contact. "We don't have any time to waste. If you know who we're looking for, I'd prefer we find him sooner rather than later."

"If you could just play the tape, I'll know him when I see him." She would never forget what he looked like, and it wasn't just because they had watched him walk out of Junior's or because she saw him on his porch. She would never forget the scruffy face, the pointy chin, and the shadowed eyes because it had shaken something in her. Frank Wilds exuded evil, even from a distance. His aura exploded with tamped down rage and secrecy. It would never be something she could explain; it was just a presence he gave off.

Sheila turned back around and started scrolling through different time stamps. She found the marker they were looking for and pushed play.

"Can you play this at an increased speed?" She hoped she didn't sound as impatient as she felt.

"Sure."

People started rapidly moving in and out of the store. There was nothing unusual, people feeding their coffee cravings, having discussions, using computers, reading, just another day at a coffee shop. The only thing that was glaringly missing from the tape was Frank Wilds.

"Dammit."

Sheila slumped, visibly disappointed that Lucy's idea didn't pan out into anything usable. "I thought we would find something."

"Me too." She touched Sheila's shoulder. "I'm sorry."

"Thank you for helping. It's easier, you know, knowing people really are looking for her." She wiped away a few tears and stood. "Guess I'd better get back to work."

They walked back out to the front of the store, and one of the baristas held out an envelope. "Someone left this for you."

"Have a good day." Lucy turned to leave but stopped short when the barista moved toward her.

"No," the barista said. "It's for you. You're Lucy, right?"

Lucy was utterly confused but she took the envelope. "Who gave this to you?"

The barista shrugged. "Some kid brought it in."

A kid? She started out the door, opening the envelope. The message was typed and concise.

Lovely piece in the paper this morning, Lucy. I didn't realize you were such a fan. I'll reach out later, so please, stay close.

The blood pumping through her veins went ice cold. Her first instinct was to look around, to see if she could catch a glimpse of Frank Wilds. But she fought the impulse, certain she wouldn't see him, though he was probably watching her. She also didn't want him to know the effect his words were having on her. No, she wouldn't give him the satisfaction. She walked over to the patio table she and Sheila had been at not long before and texted Diego to come and get her. She could've walked back to the police station to get her car, but she needed to be with her brother and Erica right now. She made sure not to let the fear she was feeling show on her face.

She sipped her now cold coffee, willing her hands not to shake. She mentally tried to picture the farthest place in town Erica and Diego could be and how long it would take to get to her. Regardless of where they were, it shouldn't be more than five to six minutes. While she waited, she pretended to play on her phone, attempting to be as carefree and unfazed as possible. When the car finally did pull up, she walked over and got into the backseat.

"What's with the 911 text?" Diego asked from the driver's seat.

Lucy handed Erica the letter, unable to keep her hands from shaking any longer.

Erica opened it and read it quickly before handing it to Diego. "What the fuck?"

"Yeah, my sentiments exactly." Being in the police cruiser with her brother and Erica was the only place she wanted to be at the moment. She had always prided herself on being brave. She thought after her time in the Middle East there was nothing that could shake her to her core. That is, until the day she was handed a letter from a serial killer.

CHAPTER TWENTY-FIVE

You aren't going on another stakeout." Erica heard herself say aloud, even though she could tell by the look on Lucy's face that her statement fell on deaf ears.

"I agree with Chance. It's not safe." Thankfully, Diego backed her up, and Lucy might listen to her brother, if not to Erica.

"Not safe? I'll be sitting next to an armed police officer and you'll be ten feet away with another armed police officer. How much safer would you like it to be?"

Erica hated that she had a point, and after reading the little message, she didn't want Lucy out of her sight. Sitting right next to her was actually exactly where she wanted her. "Fine."

Lucy looked confused. "Fine?"

"Yeah, fine. You can come with us tonight. But no more stories. You got his attention, and now we know he's watching, and local. That's what we needed."

"I'm going to write another piece. It worked. We're drawing him out, and he'll make a mistake. Then we'll be able to find Jessica and catch him." She crossed her arms to make her point.

"You aren't a cop. You aren't trained for this," Erica said, exasperated.

"I don't plan on putting the cuffs on him myself. But if I can write a piece insinuating we're onto him, that we're watching, we'll force his hand."

Diego put both hands flat down on the desk and leaned forward. "And what if you force his hand and he kills Jessica?"

Lucy flinched but acknowledged the point. "I don't think that's what's going to happen. He thinks he's smarter than us; he likes the game. He gave me the letter to taunt me because I've piqued his interest."

"Great," Diego said sarcastically. "I don't like this. I'm not using my sister as bait."

"Well, big brother, I don't need your permission."

"You're so damn stubborn." He rubbed the back of his neck.

"You are stubborn." Erica shrugged.

"Yeah well, you're tall," Lucy said.

"What?" Erica asked, feeling flustered.

"You're tall. I thought we were playing a game where we pointed out the obvious."

"This isn't a game, Lucy. All we're doing tonight is picking up a glass, or whatever else he leaves in plain sight, to get a print. If it's left in plain sight, in public, we aren't breaking any laws. Then we hope and pray we can match it to the partial we lifted off Teresa's car. The idea of all of us being there is to make him uncomfortable so he'll leave us a breadcrumb. It has to be something we see him touch and get to before anyone else does so it isn't contaminated. He doesn't know we know who he is yet, so we've got a chance of grabbing something if he's cocky. We just have to hope us being there doesn't spook him into thinking we *do* think it's him. Then we could lose him."

"Yeah, Chance, I heard the plan the first three times we went over it. It doesn't change the fact that I'm going with you." Lucy crossed her arms, her chin lifted defiantly.

"Well, I'm reminding you because you seem to be focused on the story, and we're trying to lock him up. We're not worried about what goes in your newspaper."

Erica had leaned closer to her to make her point. Lucy, in her usual style, didn't back down. "I got it, boss." She looked down at her phone and turned it around to show Erica. "Mom is here to pick me up."

"I'll pick you up at six," Erica said to Lucy's retreating figure. "Don't go anywhere on your own."

"It's a date."

"It's not a—" Erica tried to say, but Lucy was already gone.

"She's a pistol," Diego said, chuckling.

"She's impossible."

"The good ones usually are."

A few hours later, Erica pulled up in front of the Rodriguez house to pick up Lucy. As she jogged down the front porch of her parents' house, Erica was momentarily transported back to several years before. This habit of picking up Lucy for a night out was a practiced and familiar routine. That's what she told herself anyway, when she felt the excitement of seeing Lucy descend the steps warm her stomach. It was nothing more than old memories tugging at her subconscious. *Now isn't the time to fall down the rabbit hole.*

"Hi," she said as she climbed in.

"I can't believe you're actually on time," Erica joked as Lucy shut the passenger door.

"I managed to break a few bad habits over the years." She adjusted the seat, sliding it back and forth.

"I'm glad. Your lack of punctuality always drove me crazy."

"I know. But what you didn't realize was that I loved driving you crazy." She found the position she had been searching for and clicked her seat belt.

"I know."

She had always appreciated Lucy's ability to leave minor disagreements in the past. She never had any desire to rehash every point on which they didn't agree. And it appeared that luckily, she hadn't given up this attribute along with her punctuality issues. Their earlier conversation had been set aside, and although Erica was still confused and a little pissed off, she knew it was better to leave it alone and move on. She could feel Lucy's eyes on her. It felt good to be on the receiving end of Lucy's stare. She had spent so long trying to erase that particular feeling from her memory and now it seemed to reemerge, making her body tingle. She wondered if this was how it would always be, if Lucy would always be able to affect her with something as simple as a look. Was that the power your first love would always have over you? *Someone should probably put a pamphlet together, warning teenagers about the lasting effects.* She laughed at herself for being silly enough to think anyone would be brave enough to read that pamphlet before it really mattered.

"What's so funny?"

"I was just thinking. If you'd known how things would turn out, you know, with us, would you take it back?"

Lucy responded without hesitation. "Never."

Erica shot her a sideways glance. "Never?"

"The only thing I'd change about our time together was how foolish I was to end it. If I could tell anything to my twenty-year-old self, that would be it."

Erica's heart lurched at her words. She wanted to believe Lucy, desperately wanted to fall into her words and never look back. But she wasn't that person anymore, she'd grown up, and words couldn't erase everything that had happened.

She fought every instinct in her body to pull the car over and put her mouth on top of Lucy's, knowing full well she didn't need that kind of complication in her life anymore. She also needed to be on top of her game, totally focused. "Stay close tonight."

"Got it, boss."

The bar was relatively busy for a weeknight. There were a few open tables, and as they walked in, Lucy followed Erica over to one in the corner. Diego and another police officer were on the opposite end, already seated. Lucy instinctively reached out for Erica's arm when they walked through a group of people, and to her surprise, Erica let her take it in a natural and fluid movement.

She had thought they were going to have a breakthrough in the car, but Erica managed to turn off whatever she had been feeling. Lucy didn't blame her, and she wasn't going to make up for all the lost time in a matter of a few days. That type of thing only happened in romantic comedies, and her life was far from a cheesy rom-com.

"What can I get you two to drink?" The server put menus down in front of them.

"Water for me." Erica looked to Lucy.

"I'll take a glass of the house red." She had no intention of getting drunk, but she was nervous about being in the same room with Frank Wilds and needed to take the edge off. However, this was something she had no intention of sharing with Erica.

After the server had walked away, Erica said, "You realize the house red here is probably boxed wine."

Lucy shrugged. "I like to live dangerously."

"I do remember that about you."

"Oh my God, do you remember when your grandpa caught us in the front seat of my car?"

"I was just thinking about it the other day."

"You were?"

"Yeah, I remember how much it sucked to have dinner with him and your family that night. It was so awkward."

Lucy found herself flushing at the memory. "It was worth it."

A faint smile played across Erica's mouth. "It was."

The server came over and put their drinks down in front of them. "Are you ready to order?"

"Can we get an order of the chicken nachos?" Lucy asked.

The server was gone once again, and Erica shook her head. "We're working."

"We have to blend in. You already stick out like a sore thumb."

"Lucy, every single person here knows I'm a cop."

"Yeah, especially with that attitude. But that doesn't mean you need to look like you're working, does it? Isn't that the point?" Lucy was enjoying the banter and the way it made Erica smile and relax. There was still so much she wanted to tell her, so much she wanted to say, but she also wanted to hold on to this moment for as long as possible.

"He passed away a few years ago."

So much for that. "Yeah, I know. I'm sorry I couldn't come home for the funeral."

"It's okay. He asked about you pretty often, though."

Lucy wanted to sink into the floor. She'd always really loved Erica's grandfather, but she was in Iraq when he had passed. "He was a wonderful man."

"You know, he cut out every article you ever wrote. He had an online subscription to your newspaper and would print out everything to put in a scrapbook."

Lucy was beside herself. She had always assumed Erica's grandpa held on to some form of resentment for the way things had ended between them. It was a huge relief to know that wasn't the case. "That's so incredibly sweet."

"I'll have to show them to you."

"I would like that." What Lucy liked more was the idea of Erica hanging on to a scrapbook with all her articles tucked away somewhere in her house.

Lucy watched Erica's eyes, still surprised that after all these years, she still saw the same young woman she had given her heart to years ago. Those eyes tracked her now, not the way they once did, filled with wonder and excitement, but with trepidation and uncertainty. Lucy wasn't sure if the years of being a police officer had changed the way she watched people or if was just her. But the intensity was still there, and Lucy convinced herself she would enjoy it all the same, regardless of the underlying factors.

She looked like she wanted to say something, but the moment passed when Erica's eyes flicked past her and on to something or someone behind her. "There he is."

Lucy knew better than to turn and look. Erica's body tensed, and Lucy saw the muscles in her jaw flexing. Lucy wanted to touch her, to soothe her anxiety, but it wasn't her place, and it sure as hell wasn't the time.

❖

He wasn't entirely sure what they were up to, but if they thought for a moment he didn't see them all here, watching, waiting for him, they were sorely mistaken. The adrenaline he felt coursing through his veins was intoxicating, and he wondered, not for the first time, why he had avoided this game for so long.

Sure, they had their assumptions, their ideas of what he had done, if he had Jessica, but they had no proof. And in this wonderful country, an assumption was worth nothing. It was invigorating to stand here, in the middle of a busy bar, and just go about his business. He felt the invisible cloak of justice wrap around him, a protective barrier.

A somewhat plump middle-aged man sauntered to the bar. He slid his credit card across the shellacked surface and nodded to the line of draft beer handles. "What do you recommend?"

He detested this question. People seeking out the likes or dislikes of others before settling on their own always irritated him. But he needed this fucking job, so he plastered a smile on his face and walked over to the handles and poured the man a glass of their darkest beer.

He slid it back over to him. "You look like a guy who could handle this." He didn't actually think this man would like the beer, in fact, he knew he would hate it. But adding that he could *handle it* would guarantee he wouldn't come back and complain. No man ever wanted his masculinity questioned.

He noticed a group of young women over in the corner. They were sipping their pink drinks and laughing. The blonde flipped her hair off her shoulder, obviously trying to entice every man within a ten-foot radius. *Disgusting.* He did his best to temper his rage. He loathed women that acted in that manner. Trying to draw men in, just to turn them away at their first opportunity. But now wasn't the time to seem affected or even interested. There were eyes on him. *And I've got Jessica now. No need to give a fuck about the other women anymore.*

He looked over at the other two bartenders manning their respective stations. He tossed the towel down on the bar top and nodded at the manager. "I'm gonna take a smoke break." As invigorating as it was to mess with the police and show them how inept they were, it was also irritating they'd come to think of him as a suspect. *Unless they just think I can lead them to Lance. Maybe they think it's him.* He hated being unsure about things. Maybe he should take Jessica and get out while he could, just in case. He'd wanted to bring her a gift, but maybe it wasn't meant to be. He stared at Lucy Rodriguez as he walked past and felt a tingle travel up his spine. *Then again, maybe it was fate.*

❖

As soon as he disappeared out the back door, Erica walked over to the man sitting at the small table by himself. "How are you doing tonight?"

He shrugged and motioned to his glass. "Have you ever tasted this shit? It's terrible."

"Is it? Let me get you something else."

He considered this for a moment before handing the glass over. "Okay, thanks."

She took the glass from him, carefully grabbing the bottom, trying to leave as few of her fingerprints as possible. Before she walked out, she stopped at the bar and ordered the man a light beer and threw a ten down. She didn't want him complaining to the bartender, and tipping their hand. Once she made it out the door, she dumped the beer and slid the glass into a plastic bag.

She thought about going back to her seat. She could wait out the rest of the night, to make sure Frank didn't think they were on to him. Then again, he was arrogant enough to believe they had just gone home. He would think he was too smart to give anything away. He'd gotten away with everything for so long, able to live his life without repercussions, he wouldn't expect that to change now. Plus, time was a precious commodity with Jessica missing. She needed every advantage she could get.

She took a moment to make sure her face registered nothing out of the ordinary. She moved outside and to her car quickly but made sure she was cognizant of anyone who could be looking her way. Once the outside air hit her face, there was instant relief. The cool night air helped blow away the tension, leaving only the thrill of the hunt in place. This could finally be the break they needed.

CHAPTER TWENTY-SIX

"Will you be able to pull a print off that?"

Erica turned on her lights and started to back up. "If anyone can pull a print, it's Stein. But she won't be in until tomorrow morning, so it will have to wait."

"That woman from processing?" Lucy had a bit of snark in her voice.

"She's very good at her job." Erica tried not to laugh at the unwarranted jealousy woven into Lucy's words. But if she was being honest, she did enjoy it a bit.

"I'm sure she is."

Erica continued down the streets of Clearbrook, heading in the direction of the Rodriguez home. Lucy touched her arm. "I don't want to go home yet."

"Where would you like to go?"

"Can we go back to your place for a bit?"

Erica tensed. She wasn't sure what the right answer should be. On the one hand, she wanted to spend more time with Lucy. On the other, she was afraid if she did, her resolve would falter.

"Just for a drink."

Erica had never been able to say no to Lucy, and it appeared as if that was another aspect of their relationship that wasn't going to change. "Okay."

Erica pushed open her door a few minutes later, and was greeted by her waddling hound. Bella did her best to dance with excitement, but her short legs and extra ten pounds made her look more like a wobbling toy than happy pet. But to Erica's surprise, Bella's excitement wasn't directed at her entrance, but rather, at the sight of Lucy. "I have fed you every day of your life and you run right to her?"

Bella, unfazed by the accusation, turned her butt toward Lucy's hand for a good scratch.

"It's just because she can tell I'm a sucker," Lucy said as she did Bella's bidding.

"Watch out for that one. Her motives aren't pure," Erica joked.

Lucy froze. "Which one of us are you talking about?"

Erica realized how harsh her words sounded, even though they weren't intended for her. She softened her voice. "I was talking about Bella."

Lucy started toward the kitchen, seemingly embarrassed by her assumption. "Do you have any red?"

"In the wine rack."

Erica kicked off her shoes and sat on the couch. Lucy came out of the kitchen a few moments later, holding two glasses. She handed Erica one and took a seat next to her, pulling off her own shoes.

Erica desperately wanted a safe subject, and she mentally flipped through topics in her head until she landed on one. "Grayson decided to stay around for a while?"

Lucy rolled her eyes. "Yeah, he wants to go to Napa with my parents and MJ."

"You don't approve?"

"It's not that. I just don't really understand why."

"I think sometimes you forget how amazing your family is. Not everyone had the parents and brothers you did growing up." Erica wanted Lucy to see that she was lucky to have people who cared about her so much.

Lucy let the tip of her finger slide around the rim of her glass, and Erica forced herself not to stare. "Yeah, I guess I've taken them for granted sometimes."

"Plus, it's not like MJ is bad to look at."

Lucy scrunched her nose in mock disgust. "Ew. But I don't see why that would matter. He's straight."

Erica sipped her wine and purposely avoided eye contact. She had never been a good liar, and that was multiplied when it came to Lucy.

Lucy grabbed her arm. "Chance, what aren't you telling me?"

Erica shrugged. "How do you know he's straight?"

Lucy gripped her arm tighter. "Oh, I don't know, maybe the parade of women he's enjoyed his entire life."

"All I'm saying is, maybe there are things you don't know about your brother." She was talking about MJ, but her mind was on the way Lucy's hand felt on her arm.

"And you do?"

"I talk to him at least once a week." She focused on Lucy, trying to stay on the track of their conversation.

"You do?" Lucy was visibly hurt.

"You could too. You just have to call him." She wanted to point out how many issues could be solved if Lucy was willing to communicate, but she wasn't sure she wanted to open that particular can of memories.

Lucy took a big gulp from her wine glass. "I'm terrible at staying in touch."

"So, change it." Lucy let go of her arm, and Erica was surprised that she immediately missed the contact.

"I need to, I just…I don't know. I had a really hard time there for a while, after coming back."

Erica let Lucy continue to work out her thoughts. She was curious as to why she'd steered clear of her family for so long when they'd been so close.

"It was difficult for me to relate to people. They always had so many questions about what happened, how I felt, if I was proud of my story. It was so crazy for people to ask me that, as if that's all it boiled down to, a stupid award. They cared about what happened after, and I felt like I was trapped in that day over and over. I saw it when I went to sleep, when I heard a car backfire, even certain smells set me off."

Erica had wished several times since she had found out about what happened that she had sent the letter she had written Lucy, but never more than she did in this moment. "I'm so sorry you had to go through that. I'm even more sorry you went through it alone."

"The alone part was my choice, and therapy has helped. But I couldn't handle my family asking those same questions, because I couldn't blow them off the way I could other people's questions, you know? I'd have to be real with them, and there was just no way. And now I'm realizing how much I've missed."

"Are you still seeing a therapist?"

Lucy laughed. "Yes, and I probably always will." She moved closer to Erica. Their legs were touching, and Erica could do nothing but stare at the place they touched.

"But what I really wanted was for you to hold me and tell me everything was going to be okay."

For the first time in a long time, Erica didn't think about her actions or the aftermath. She was always deliberate in her dealings with women, wanting to take the safest path possible to avoid heartbreak for both parties. But the emotions that were pushing down her thoughts, drowning her rational brain, were overwhelming.

She leaned over, hesitating a millimeter from Lucy's lips. She could feel her breath on her lips, sweet with wine and longing. She knew Lucy wouldn't close the last miniscule amount of distance between them. Lucy wanted this to be her choice. So she made it, putting her mouth against hers.

Erica intended for the kiss to be brief, a confirmation that feelings still existed, regardless of what they meant. But intentions only work for people who have already determined what they truly want. Erica let the rush of being held captive by Lucy's draw wash over her, just as it had twelve years ago.

She felt Lucy's hands touch her face, soft and trembling. The realization that Lucy was as overwhelmed by the current running between the two of them as she was, was the last nudge she needed. She pulled her closer and felt Lucy's chest heave against her own. She needed air but didn't want to break the connection.

Lucy's hands slid down her back to the bottom of her shirt and pulled it free. Her hands felt like cool liquid against her heating body and were a welcome relief. An involuntary shiver traveled over her skin as Lucy's hands roamed over her. Lucy drew Erica's shirt up over her head. Once free of the material, she fell backward, pulling Lucy down with her. With the weight of Lucy's body on top of her, Erica gave herself over to the moment. Every nerve ending sparked and sizzled with a primal craving for Lucy.

Lucy seemed to feel it too. She broke their fevered contact to take off her own shirt. When their bare skin came into contact, Lucy let a guttural moan escape her lips, further exciting Erica's already growing desire. The next several minutes passed in a frenzied reunion of kissing, touching, and rediscovering. Erica only let her mind briefly hover over the fact that Lucy was now much more experienced, more practiced than she had been the last time they had been together. The unfamiliarity fueled a sense of possessiveness inside her that she hadn't experienced with anyone since Lucy.

Erica slid her hands between them, unbuttoning Lucy's jeans, sliding her hands down her body, and taking the garment with them. Lucy slid her legs out and repositioned herself on top of Erica, straddling her waist. Erica was mesmerized by the way Lucy felt and the contours of her face in the dim light of her living room. The way her head still seemed to fit perfectly against her neck as she nibbled and kissed the exposed skin.

Lucy pushed her middle harder and harder into Erica's stomach, and the wetness Erica could feel was pushing her own arousal toward the edge. She moved her hand down Lucy's bare stomach. She finally let her thumb rest against where she knew Lucy's clitoris hid behind her thin underwear. She put a small amount of pressure against it, feeling Lucy's body tremble, her hands squeezing her shoulders as if she was trying to stall the orgasm building inside her.

Erica moved her thumb slowly as Lucy's hips pushed harder and faster against her. She only sped up when the whimpers began to escape Lucy's mouth, becoming more desperate with each stroke. Erica pushed harder, causing Lucy's body to grow rigid, and a cry of relief and desperation fell from her. Then she felt Lucy's hands circling her neck. She placed soft wet kisses up and down her cheek and neck.

Lucy spoke into her ear, barely above a whisper. "I've spent years missing the way you touch me."

Her words, their meaning, was something they were going to have to explore later. Right now, all she wanted was to stay in this place with Lucy, protected from the things that had happened and the time they had missed.

Lucy reached for Erica's jeans just as her phone rang. Erica reached for it, blindly feeling her pockets.

"Don't answer that."

"I have to. It could be important."

"This is important." She continued to kiss her neck.

"Not as important as Jessica." She put the phone up to her ear. "Detective Chance."

A part of Erica wanted to stay right here, in this moment with Lucy. She wanted this night to continue. She wanted to let Lucy continue her exploration. She didn't understand what all of that meant right now. She didn't know if this was something she really wanted, to drop back down the rabbit hole. But she hadn't been thinking about those things. Her brain was fuzzy with arousal and excitement. But the other part of her knew that if she didn't take a phone call, it could be *the* phone call. It could be the discovery or link they needed for this case. That possibility couldn't be risked for anything, regardless of what her body was telling her.

CHAPTER TWENTY-SEVEN

Thanks for coming in to see if you can pull prints." Erica leaned against the doorframe, talking to Stein.

"Of course. When Diego told me you managed to get something, I didn't want to waste any time. You should have called." She smiled at Erica, which irritated Lucy.

Lucy walked over to the table and looked over Stein's shoulder. "How's this work, anyway?" She didn't want to listen to the subtle flirting between Erica and Stein. They hadn't talked about what had happened between them. Lucy wasn't sure what it meant for either of them, but she did know she didn't like Stein drooling all over Erica.

Stein pulled gloves over her hands and pulled the glass from the bag. "Simple really. I use ninhydrin and physical developer to reveal latent fingerprints. These chemicals react with specific components of latent print residue, such as amino acids and inorganic salts. Ninhydrin causes prints to turn a purple color, which makes them easy to photograph. Once I can photograph them, I can process them, then we put them in the system and see if they match the partial I lifted."

"Yeah, simple." Diego chuckled from the corner.

"This will actually go a bit faster if people don't hover." She looked at Lucy expectantly.

Lucy sighed and took a seat next to Erica. Erica stared at Stein as if willing her to move at light speed. Lucy took the time to study Erica's profile, the beautiful lines of her neck, the small scar on her cheek from falling off her bike when they were kids, and her wonderful blue eyes. Her eyes had always been one of Lucy's favorite features. They reminded her of the sky, subtly changing. Sometimes, they would be pure and crystal, other times they would be a bit dark and stormy. *How could you have ever been so stupid? You should have never let her go. But what now? Do I really want this? Do I want to put Erica through this if I'm not absolutely sure?*

"This is going to take me an hour or two, so feel free to go somewhere else. Somewhere not here," Stein said without turning around.

Diego pushed himself off the wall he was leaning against. "I'm going to head home." He clapped his hands. "Hopefully, we get a hit and can get a warrant first thing in the morning."

Erica turned and looked at her. "Want to go get a cup of coffee?"

"I'd like that."

"I'll take mine with cream and two sugars," Stein called as they were walking out.

"I know how you take your coffee," Erica called back.

Once they were in her car, Lucy had to know how Erica knew the way Stein took her coffee. "Did you sleep with her?"

"Who?" Erica looked surprised by the question.

"Stein." She kept her voice flat, without accusation.

"Stein? No, why?"

"She has a crush on you. And you know how she takes her coffee."

Erica looked between the road and Lucy. "You can't seriously be jealous."

"I was just pointing out a fact." She didn't want to come off as defensive, as if she had some claim to Erica. But she needed to know all the same. She needed to know how many romantic connections Erica had in the town, since it could complicate things if they did move forward.

"Lucy, even if I had slept with her, it's not really any of your business."

Lucy knew that. She hated that it was the truth, but she knew it. She reached out to touch Erica's leg and Erica flinched. "I know it's not." Erica's tone had been a bit harsh, like something else was bothering her. "Is everything okay?"

Erica's jaw clenched. "Look, I don't regret what happened, back at my house. But let's not get ahead of ourselves."

Lucy crossed her arms, trying to protect herself from Erica's words and sensing a caveat coming. "Well, what a relief."

Erica spared her a glance but just barely. "I just don't know what it means. Just because we're still attracted to each other, it doesn't change the past."

"What are you saying? You don't think there's a chance for us?"

"I don't know. There's too much behind us, and it doesn't change where we are in our lives now, does it? You're a hotshot journalist with big awards working in a big city. You're not about to give that up to come back to your small-town roots, are you?" She shrugged and her eyes were damp. "You'll leave again, because we live in different worlds now. Maybe we always did, and it just took time to figure that out."

Lucy felt the weight of Erica's words in her chest. She felt like she was suffocating, the words squeezing her lungs, taking the wind out of her. "Pull over." She wasn't sure what she wanted, but it felt like Erica had just taken the decision away from her. *With the truth.* It sounded final, and Lucy wasn't ready for final.

"No. I'm not going to leave you on the side of the road."

"Dammit, Erica, pull the car over."

Erica did as she was told, and the car slowed to a halt. Lucy jumped out, then slammed the car door. "I'll walk home."

"That's crazy. Get in the car."

"I can't be around you right now. I'm embarrassed and I'm upset. I need to walk."

Erica leaned out the window, her eyes intense and determined. "You can't walk around. Don't be ridiculous. You can't be reckless just because something didn't go your way." She got out of the car now and pulled the door open. "Get in."

"I'm thirty-two years old and I've managed to survive for twelve years without you. I think I can handle one more mile." She forced herself not to look at Erica as she kept walking.

Her words had their desired effect. Erica got back in the car and pulled away, leaving her alone again.

Lucy crossed her arms and marched down the street. She was hurt and she felt like she was losing Erica all over again. Erica had dismissed her so easily. *Is that how she felt when I left?* She was replaying the scene over in her head. The clarity of the last five minutes was acute, even through her tears. She didn't see the bushes in front of her shift until he was standing right in front of her, and his hand was coming toward her face. She tried to scream, but the fumes stole her voice as she fell into darkness.

Erica's phone rang, and she pulled it out of her pocket, hoping it was Lucy. She felt terrible about what happened and wanted to make sure she had gotten home okay. She was surprised to see Sheila's name on her screen.

"Hey, Sheila. Everything okay?"

"Just checking to see if there is any news."

"I'll let you know as soon as there's anything concrete." The last thing she wanted to do was give her any false hope.

"How are things with Lucy?"

There was no commitment between Sheila and Erica, but she felt the least she could do was offer her closure, if she needed it. "Sheila, you know I care about you—"

"Save it, Chance. I don't need you to break up with me. We spent time together, we had a good time, but we both knew it wasn't going anywhere. I'm happy being friends."

Well, this is a first. "Are you sure?" She felt more relieved than she probably should have. Sheila was going through a hard time right now, and Erica didn't want to cause her more pain.

"Don't be such a girl."

Erica laughed. "This would be the first time I've been accused of being too emotional in a relationship."

"I like breaking records. What happened with Lucy?"

"Nothing." Sheila might have said she wanted to be friends, but it felt a bit weird to be having this conversation with the woman she had been seeing up until about two seconds ago.

"You freaked out?"

"Why would you say that?" She traced the steering wheel with her thumb. She wondered if she had always been this transparent or if it only applied to Lucy.

"Seriously? Because that's what you do."

"If I do, it's only because of what Lucy did to me twelve years ago."

"Oh, Jesus." Sheila drew out the last part of the word.

"What?" She wasn't sure if Sheila was accusing her of something or pointing out something she had missed.

"When are you going to own your bullshit? Yes, Lucy broke your heart, but everything you've done since then has been your choice. You chose to create this little wall around yourself. Lucy didn't do that to you. She made a choice a zillion years ago. You were the one who chose to hang on to her and not let anyone else in. Eventually, though, people change, and they realize what's important to them. Unfortunately, it's usually not until they've lost it. Maybe she's at that stage. The question is, are you?"

"I can't go through it again. I can't risk it." Her muscle memory kicked in, and she felt a pang in her chest of what all those months had been like after Lucy.

"Then I feel sorry for you. Because if you won't risk it, then how will you ever win?"

"You sound like a fortune cookie." Erica smiled, hoping she could hear the appreciation for the counsel in her voice.

"I've had some time to reevaluate my priorities." She sighed. "I'll call you."

"Okay, and, Erica, don't be an idiot. Not everyone gets a second chance."

Erica laughed.

"See what I did there?"

"Yeah, like I haven't heard it before. Bye, Sheila."

She tossed the phone down in the empty seat that Lucy had occupied not long before. She knew there was some truth to what Sheila had said. *Okay, a lot of truth.* Erica had used what happened between her and Lucy as a shield from things and people that had the potential to hurt her. *But where has that gotten me?* She hadn't achieved some supreme level of happiness, impervious from anything bad happening. The only thing it had ever really gotten her was solitude. But that didn't change where they were in their lives. Lucy lived eight hundred miles away. She had an entire life that didn't include Erica. A life that hadn't included her for years. Was that something she would change? Erica wasn't sure she wanted the truth.

CHAPTER TWENTY-EIGHT

L ucy's brain was foggy, her head hurt, and she was struggling to make her limbs move. She was starting to get the feeling back in her arms when she realized they were lying in a damp, cool, crumbly material. She was trying to make her brain process the familiar texture, but it wasn't until her eyes came into focus that she was able to ascertain she was lying in dirt.

She pushed herself up, struggling to hold her body weight up with one arm. *What the fuck happened?* The place was dark, but there was a naked light bulb barely illuminating her surroundings.

"Are you okay?" a whisper came from a corner of the room.

She tried to get up quickly, but she lacked the body coordination at the moment. "Who said that?"

"He won't be back for a few hours. He won't sleep down here."

Lucy rubbed her head and crawled toward the voice. When she finally reached her, she recognized her immediately. "Jessica."

Jessica grabbed her arms and pulled her up against the wall. "I'm sorry. I would've helped you, but—"

"It's okay. Are you okay?"

Jessica shook her head. "I'm trying to be, but it gets harder every day." Tears fell from her eyes, streaking the smudges of dirt on her face. "I don't know what he wants. He has some weird notion that we're meant to be together."

"Do you know him from somewhere?" She already knew the answer but wasn't sure if Jessica had figured it out yet.

She nodded. "I used to date his cousin. I just didn't realize who he was at first."

"The police are on to him. We're going to get out of here."

Jessica grabbed her arms again, frantic. "You have to play along, no matter what he says. If you don't, he'll kill you. I watched him do it." She sobbed. "Please, just promise me you won't do anything to upset him."

Lucy wrapped an arm around her, pulling her close. "We're going to get out of here. I promise, we're both getting out of here." She knew these things because she knew Erica and Diego. She knew they'd find her; she believed it in her bones. And instincts were what kept reporters alive.

Jessica tucked her head into her shoulder, her body shaking. "He's coming."

"How do you know?"

A moment later, the door screeched, the sound of steel on steel. Footsteps descended the stairs, slow and heavy.

"You didn't think I'd go to bed without saying good night, did you?"

He walked over and reached for Jessica's face, and she let him touch it. "I told you I'd bring you a present. Do you like it?"

Jessica tucked her head back against Lucy.

He grabbed her face and turned it back toward him, his voice was calm. "I asked you a question."

Lucy could hear the chatter of Jessica's teeth. "Yes, thank you."

He let her face go, forcefully pushing it to the side. "See, was that so hard?"

He squatted in front of them now. Lucy didn't think she had the strength to get them both out of here if she did manage to kick him in the face hard enough to knock him out.

He ticked his finger back and forth. "I know what you're thinking. I've seen the look before. You wouldn't make it out of here, and even if you did, she wouldn't." He nodded in Jessica's direction.

"What exactly do you want?"

"With you? You're going to write my story. Then, when it's perfect, I'm going to kill you. So it would behoove you to write with as much detail and as accurately as possible."

"And if I refuse?" Lucy tried to sit up as straight as her body would allow.

"You won't." He reached over and tapped on her chest. Lucy tried to move away, but there was nowhere to go. Her back was literally against a wall. "If you refuse, you're going to make me hurt Jessica until you finally give in. I don't want to do that, and I'm sure you don't want to watch that."

Lucy didn't have anything to say because she knew he was right. She thought back to the blazing desert of the Middle East and the moment she'd held her friend's hand as he'd taken his last breaths. She couldn't do anything to save him, but she could save Jessica. All she needed to do was play along until Diego and Erica found them. She could play his sick little game.

He moved back toward the steel door he had entered through. He had a skip in his step, so proud of himself. "I'll see you ladies bright and early."

The loud hinges screamed and then she was alone again with Jessica. Her trembling body and quiet sobs were the only proof there was anything left in her. Lucy knew, even if they did survive this, Jessica would never be the same. This place would haunt her dreams and every quiet thought she had for the rest of her life. Lucy couldn't change that now, but she could make sure there was a life to lead.

She squeezed Jessica. "It's going to be okay. The cops know it's him. They're going to get him."

"I thought the same thing, but then no one came."

"They'll come."

"How do you know?" She played with a loose string on her shirt.

"You heard him. I wrote a story about him. They'll know he took me."

"So they know it's him? They know it's specifically him?" Excitement shined in her eyes.

"It's only a matter of time. You have to trust me. They're going to find us."

She didn't want to tell Jessica everything she knew. She wasn't sure she could keep it to herself, under these circumstances. She had been down here for days, she wasn't in her right mind, and she could give something away without meaning to. Plus, she wasn't sure how to explain her connection to Erica. She didn't want to tell her that finding Lucy would be more important to Erica than Jessica ever would be, than anything ever would be. Erica would never let anything happen to her. Erica was connected to her; she always had been. She could feel the memory of her every day, like a brand that had been burned into her heart years ago. It was a connection that tethered her to Erica and would until she ceased to exist. Those strings were never severed. They might fray, they might pull, but they never severed. She knew Erica would come for her the same way she knew the sun would rise in the morning. It was simply the way the world was designed.

CHAPTER TWENTY-NINE

E rica opened her eyes, and it took her a moment to realize where she was. It came into focus quickly, the peg board with tools hanging from metal stems, the harsh fluorescent lighting. She was in the processing center.

"What do you have?" she croaked, her voice still heavy with sleep.

Stein pushed the paper toward her. "I had to send them off to the state facility. My findings were inconclusive."

Erica stood, frustration flooding her. "What?"

"I'm sorry, Chance. I put a rush order on it and told them it involved a missing person."

Erica took in a deep breath, trying her best to control her irritation. This wasn't Stein's fault. If anything it was hers. She should have more evidence by now. *There has to be something.* "Any word when we'll know for sure? I need to get that warrant."

Stein put her hand on her arm. "You know that's going to take a bit more time."

"We don't have more time."

She left, not bothering to listen to whatever Stein was saying to her back.

A few minutes later, she was in front of the Rodriguez house. She sat out front for a few minutes, thinking about what she could say to Lucy. It wasn't that she didn't have feelings for her, she did. She always had. That was actually the problem. What if she revealed herself to Lucy again, let her back in? What would stop her from leaving again?

MJ and Grayson came walking out the front door with Holly on a leash. *Guess it's time to deal with stuff.* She got out of the car and walked around to the other side.

Grayson waved. "Morning. Where's Lucy?"

Erica felt the first pang of anxiety flush her system. "What do you mean? She's supposed to be here."

MJ scratched Holly's head. "When she didn't come home last night, we thought she was with you."

"No, I dropped her off...down the road a little way after we left the station."

Erica pulled out her phone. She called Lucy and it went straight to voice mail. The anxiety was now rapidly combining with adrenaline, rising in her body like a thermometer on a hot stove.

She called Diego, and he answered on the second ring. "Hey, Chance."

"Is Lucy with you?" *Please say yes. Please, God.*

"No, I thought she was at my parents' house."

She got back in the driver's seat. "She's not, and they haven't seen her. She's not answering her phone, either." She swallowed the bile of fear at the back of her throat. "What if he has her?"

There was silence on the other end of the phone. Diego was processing the possibility of Frank Wilds having his little sister.

"I'll be at your house in five." She pointed to Grayson and MJ. "Get your parents and go over to Diego's house. I'm going to send a police cruiser over for protection."

"Chance, what's going on?" MJ asked. "Is Lucy in trouble?"

"Just go."

She barely got the car to a complete stop when Diego hopped in. She didn't turn the siren on. She didn't want to give him any indication that they were coming. She glanced over at Diego and saw he was checking the bullets in his gun. She didn't need to say where they were headed.

"If he has her, we'll get her back."

He put the gun back in its holster and snapped it shut. "You're damn right we will."

A few minutes later, they pulled into the dusty drive. Erica's skin was tingling, and her senses were on high alert, courtesy of the adrenaline surge pulsing through her veins. After a moment, she parked the car in front of the Wildses' house.

She looked at Diego. "We still need to do this by the book."

"Which book?" Fury blazed behind his eyes.

"Look, if this asshole has Lucy, I want his head on a platter. But if we do anything to fuck this up, he's going to walk. We can't let that happen." What she really wanted to do was beat the living hell out of him until he told them where Jessica and Lucy were. She wanted to squeeze his neck until the words choked out of his throat. Luckily, she didn't say it out loud, giving Diego more ideas than he already had about torturing Frank Wilds.

They walked to the front door, a place they had just been a few days prior, unaware at the time the person they were speaking to was the man they had been looking for. He now had Lucy. He unknowingly had the power to break whatever remained of Erica's heart, once and for all.

Frank Wilds pushed the screen door open before they had a chance to knock. "Good morning, Detectives. What can I help you with today?"

Erica could feel the hatred pouring off Diego in waves, but that wouldn't get them anywhere. They didn't have sufficient evidence yet, and if Diego came unhinged, he was going to end up doing something irrational, putting them all in danger.

"We wanted to talk to you a bit more about your cousin. Can we come in?"

Frank spun an apple around in his hand, then took a bite. "I don't have a whole lot else to say. Like I told you before, he's out of town."

"But you are familiar with Jessica Vargas?"

"Yeah, I'm familiar with a lot of people in this town, Detective."

"What about Lucy Rodriguez?" Diego snarled from a foot away.

Frank took his time replying, a large smile playing across his face as he took another bite of apple. "Why? She missing too?"

Erica wanted to take the butt of her gun and smack the smug smile off his face. But this could be the opening they were looking for, the chance to trip him up. "Lucy? No, she's down at the *Clearbrook Press* right now."

He might not have felt his body stiffen and his jaw clench, but Erica saw it. Then, just like that, he slipped back under his mask. "You sure about that?"

"Are you?" Erica said.

He took another bite from his apple. "Just kinda weird to question me if you already know she's down at the *Press* office."

"Well, I just got off the phone with her. No worries. Back to Jessica."

He threw the apple into the field in front of his house and looked at Diego. "Why did you ask?"

Diego wasn't capable of playing along with Erica's game. "You know why."

Erica was just about to interject when Diego exploded. "You know what, fuck this. Franklin Wilds, you are under arrest for the murder of Teresa Ortiz." He flipped Frank around, pressing him against the front of his house. Frank didn't resist, and a wicked smile crossed his lips as he stared coldly into Erica's eyes.

Diego put the handcuffs on him and pulled him off the wall, dragging him toward the car. "You have the right to remain silent. Anything you say can and will be used against you in a court of law. You have a right to an attorney. If you cannot afford an attorney, one will be appointed for you. Do you understand these rights?"

Diego opened the car door and flipped him around. "Do you understand these rights?"

"Yes," Frank said as he slid into the back of the car. He continued to stare at Erica, chewing on the last bits of remaining apple in his mouth.

Erica glared at Diego from across the roof of the car. She wanted to see this asshole locked up as bad as he did, but they didn't have any hard evidence yet, nothing solid to give the DA. If they couldn't produce something fast, he was going to walk, and that blood would now be on their hands. They needed a miracle. They needed that partial print to match and they needed it to come back quick. That, or they needed to get Frank talking, without invoking his right to a lawyer. The only upside to this was keeping him away from Jessica and Lucy for ninety-six hours. It wasn't nearly enough, but it was something.

Lucy didn't know what time it was, but she was sure several hours had passed. She had managed to fall asleep, but it was because of exhaustion and emotional depletion. She had finally gotten complete control back of her limbs and was able to move around the small space she had been dumped in.

"I don't know why he didn't tie you up."

Lucy was picking up items on his workbench and turning them over in her hand. "He's getting cocky, overly confident. He thinks he's untouchable."

Lucy ran her hands over the brown stains on the old wooden workbench. Bloodstains he'd never bothered to clean, assuming it would never be found. The scars and nicks that marked the table, shaped like half-moons and pitted valleys, were proof of the brutality and energy put into each endeavor. On the other side of the workbench was a bucket with a small scrub brush. Lucy picked it up, wondering why he never used it to clean up the remnants of his kills.

As if reading her thoughts, Jessica answered. "He uses it to clean their nails." She was still huddled in the corner, rocking slowly back and forth.

"Hey," she said, pulling a screwdriver off one of the hooks. "We're going to get out of here." She wanted to know more. She wanted to know exactly what Jessica had seen, everything she had been privy to, but she was too fragile right now. That would have to be a conversation for a later time.

Lucy went over to the wooden staircase Frank had ascended the night before and pushed the screwdriver into one of the hinges, trying to pry it free. She could hear Jessica crying again, and she needed her to be ready to go with her if she was able to get the door off, but her current state wouldn't do. "I met your cousin Sheila."

Being reminded of her life outside the dark, dismal cave seemed to breathe a bit of life into her. "You did?"

Lucy continued to work on the hinge, trying a different angle. "I did, and she's very worried about you. Everyone is."

"How about my parents? Are they okay? What about Zack?"

Lucy hadn't actually had the chance to meet any of them, but she figured there was no point in saying so now. "They're okay. Hanging in there. They're all waiting for you. I'm sure there will be a big party."

"Zack hates parties."

"I bet he'll make an exception."

"I kind of thought Zack and I would get married. Before, well, before this."

Lucy stopped for a moment, wanting to make sure Jessica was looking at her. "Don't talk like that. This isn't over."

Jessica slowly walked over and started watching her closely. "I'm not sure I can ever go back. How will anything ever be normal again? I'm afraid this is all I will see every time I close my eyes, every time I walk to my car. What if I can never be the person he remembered, the person he loved?"

Lucy had a flash of the Middle East and everything that had happened there and since. She thought of all the sleepless nights she had spent alone with her own thoughts. She thought of the way she still had to take a deep breath when she heard a car backfire and the way her body automatically recoiled at the smell of gunpowder on the Fourth of July. She knew Jessica was going to have her own moments after this was over, and it was going to take time and tears to recover. And the truth was, she probably never would fully recover. This would become a part of her. Something she would have to deal with forever, something that she would always dream about, and something she would always remember in detail. From this point forward, she would be tied to this story, to Frank Wilds's name, and to the girls who hadn't made it.

Lucy put the screwdriver down and gently placed her hands on Jessica's shoulders. "Listen to me, you were never going to stay the exact same person he fell in love with. You were always going to change. We're meant to. It's part of the human experience. What you're going through right now will become part of you, but it will only define you if you let it. It might not seem like it right now, but you'll learn how to manage the panic attacks, how to handle the situations that mentally thrust you right back here. You'll learn how to cope with all of this because you're a fighter."

"How do you know I'm a fighter?"

"Because you've made it this far. You've adapted to whatever crazy game he's playing. You found a way to survive and you will outside of these walls too. And if Zack really loves you, he loves all of you, including that fighter."

"Thanks, Lucy. I just hope you're right."

The hinges weren't going to budge, the top and bottom had both been soldered shut, but the attempt to try to help free them was making her feel better all the same. She wasn't sure how much time she had or when Frank would be back, but she needed to do something to make her feel like she was at least trying.

"Where are we exactly?" She was trying to figure out in her mind if there was a time table she could work from. If they were under the house, he could get to them quickly. If they were somewhere else, that could benefit them.

"We're under his barn."

"Under?"

Jessica nodded. "He took me up to the house once. He let me take a shower after…" Her voice trailed off, and Lucy watched her eyes trail off to a memory.

"After what?"

"After he killed the other woman." She started crying again, but there were no sobs, just tears.

Lucy was going to push for more, but the look on Jessica's face told her to let it rest for now. This poor woman had suffered a significant amount of physical and mental distress over the last several days.

Jessica looked up at her again, and she seemed to fall on a topic she wanted to talk about. "Do you have a Zack?"

It's interesting, the way a kidnapping can bring two people together. Lucy almost laughed at the ridiculousness of it all. Two people who hardly knew each other could ask the most intimate of questions, because neither knew if they would have the opportunity to confide in anyone ever again.

"I used to. Now, I don't know. Maybe."

"Does he know you're a fighter?"

"She, and yeah, I think she knows."

If Jessica was surprised by the use of the pronoun, she didn't show it. "Good. I'm glad to hear that. Maybe if we get out of here, you can remind her."

"I'll make you a deal. *When* we get out of here, I'll make sure of it."

She had said it without thinking and was surprised by the truth her statement held. She hadn't intentionally made up her mind about the future she wanted with Erica, and yet there it was. She did want her, not just as a friend, but as her person. She didn't want pieces of Erica. She didn't want to be part of her life just to eventually see her with someone else. She wanted Erica, all of her. She didn't need closure. She needed a beginning.

CHAPTER THIRTY

Erica and Diego stood on the other side of the only interrogation room in their station. There was no need to question Diego for the choice he made. He understood the consequences, and they were a team. It didn't matter now anyway. It was time to get to work.

The chief pushed open the door. Erica called him about the arrest and he had been there within minutes. He stood on the other side of Diego, arms folded, looking intently at Frank Wilds.

"You two better know what you're doing. Jessica Vargas is still missing, you think he may have Lucy, and if you fuck this up, he'll get away with all of it." His voice was heavy and gravelly. It had always reminded Erica of the sound rocks make rolling under your shoes.

"We got it, Chief," Erica said.

"You better, Chance. There's no room for error. I'm about five minutes away from calling the FBI for help."

Diego made a move toward the door, and Erica put a hand on him. "I'll go in first. He obviously has some issues with women. Let's see how it pans out. He thinks he's smarter than me. Maybe he won't lawyer up right away."

Diego rubbed his face and nodded. "I'm here if you need me."

"I know."

She stood outside the door before going in, reminding herself to do everything by the book. Lucy, Jessica, and the cases of the other three women were at stake. She needed to be clearheaded and focused.

She wasn't sure if he would even talk to her, but she had to try, for Lucy's sake. For her own as well. If she hadn't let Lucy get out of her car, she would be here now, with her. They would be figuring this out together. She'd known she shouldn't let her walk alone, but she'd gotten pissed off and let her do it anyway. Now she was in the hands of this twisted fuck, and it was Erica's fault.

"You don't have anything on me. This is all in your head. The DA won't risk prosecution without evidence. And there is zero evidence that I'm involved in any way. You have the wrong guy."

Erica sat at the table and stared at him. His eyes were clear and focused, but there was something missing. With most people, there was emotion, whether it be fear, guilt, or apprehension when sitting in a police interrogation room. But Frank Wilds's eyes were vacant, void of anything except the fluorescent bulbs reflecting against them. She wanted to tell him they had a partial print and were just waiting for confirmation, she wanted to see if that would spur anything, but she held it back. If he knew there was actual evidence at this point, he might lawyer up, and she needed to know where to find Lucy and Jessica.

"So here's the thing, Frank. I didn't want to arrest you. I don't actually think you did this. Personally, I think it's your cousin's handiwork, and you just got caught in the middle."

"Like I told you, he hasn't been around."

Erica opened the file she had brought in with her and pulled out a picture of Teresa Ortiz and slid it in front of him. His eyes slid over the photo, an image of Teresa, pale, cold, and dead, her head caved in on one side. She slid another one in front of him, a picture of the body taken where they had found her. It had been her final resting place, a dirt road she had probably never driven down before, surrounded by people she had never met.

"Never seen her." His eyes said something different. There was a glimmer of recognition.

"See, that's what I figured. I knew my partner was making a mistake. This has Lance written all over it. I mean, these murders, they took planning and dedication. The man who did this needed to be strong, smart, and attractive enough to lure Teresa and Jessica without raising the suspicion of anyone around them."

She watched his jaw clench, a flicker of emotion showing in his eyes. *Rage.* She pulled out a picture of Claudia next, sliding it next to Teresa's. "These women are young, and whoever killed them would have had to lure them in somehow. I told my partner it wouldn't have been you. That would be crazy. I mean, no offense, but why would two twenty-somethings go anywhere with you? You're what?" She pulled up his file, pretending she didn't have it memorized. "Fifty years old?"

"It couldn't have been Lance. That newspaper article said these murders span twenty-five years. He wasn't even alive when they first happened." He sat back in his chair, a little smugger than a moment ago.

"I know. I think he's a copycat."

"That's absurd."

"Is it? Think about it. We haven't found Jessica yet, so maybe he's keeping her alive. Maybe he always felt a little burned by her, held on to a bit of animosity. He was just warming up with Claudia and Teresa, making sure he honed his skills for Jessica. The guy who killed those women years ago was obviously a one-off, since he never did it again."

As she spoke, he became more and more focused on the photos. His eyes were traveling up and down, in an almost intimate movement. She needed to push him a bit more, see where it led.

"The way Claudia was left, it was almost like he cared about her. She had been cleaned and laid on the ground like she was resting."

"Maybe whoever did this did care about her."

There it is. It might only be a slight opening, but she was going to take it. "What makes you say that?"

"Well, from this picture, her hair is out of her eyes, so he took his time to make sure that happened. She was found in the dirt, but she isn't all that dirty, so he must have carried her there. I would think someone who does that cared about the person."

"Yeah, but he killed her. That's not how you treat someone you care about."

He picked the picture up with both hands, almost reverently. His face flushed a bit, and for a moment, she thought she saw a small inkling of remorse. But just as quickly as it had come, it disappeared. His eyes once again flecked with rage. "Maybe she deserved it."

"What could she have done to deserve this?" She motioned to the picture.

"The devil has infinite ways of enacting retribution. These girls, they run around teasing men, making them think they can have something, and then pull it away from them. I can see where someone would get fed up, want to take matters into his own hands."

The way he said it, the way the words rolled off his tongue, full of self-righteousness and entitlement, sent shivers through her body. Her phone vibrated and she pulled it from her pocket. Stein was on her way over. The message said she had more bad news. "I need to take this. I'll be right back."

She walked into the adjoining room, still rubbing her arms. Diego was standing in the same place she had left him, arms still folded across his chest.

He looked at her and pointed at Frank Wilds through the window. "This sick motherfucker needs to be locked up. He's holding Jessica and Lucy, and we need to find out where they are. Who knows what he's done to them."

He was right. The thought of anything happening to Lucy was enough to make her want to throw up then and there. She had been trying to keep it out of her mind while talking to him. The only thing holding her together was the knowledge that while he was here with them, he wasn't with Jessica and Lucy.

Stein walked into the room, a look of defeat on her face. Erica knew what she was going to say before the words came out of her mouth. "The prints are inconclusive."

Erica felt the blood drain from her head. This was not the outcome she had been hoping for. She wanted solid evidence in her hand. She fought the impulse to sit, not wanting to give in to the heavy feeling of failure.

Years started to flash before her eyes. She pictured nights and days in a world where Lucy no longer existed. An infinite line that stretched on and on, with dimmed colors, without taste, without anything real. A world without Lucy wasn't a place she ever wanted to exist. Even when they had been apart, just knowing she was out there somewhere brought her a sense of peace. An alternative to that reality wasn't something she could live with.

She looked at the chief, who hadn't yet offered an idea or an alternative to their situation. He stood with his hand over his mouth, staring contemplatively at the monster they finally had trapped, in their grasp, and would have to let go. Sure, at this point, she could come up with something flimsy to search the property, but she wouldn't get access to all of it. And then if they didn't find what they were looking for, he would be in the wind, the fate of Jessica and Lucy out of her control.

No, she wasn't going to let any of that happen. Playing by the rules hadn't gotten them anywhere yet. They needed to do something different.

"Let him go."

"What?" Diego yelled at her. "No. No fucking way."

"I'm going to go out to the property. I'll wait for him there. He's going to go to them. I know he will. He'll need to see them." She kept her voice calm, to prove her plan made sense.

"And then what?"

"And then I'll take him in once I've seen where he's keeping them. It's a stakeout with a clear purpose. Nothing illegal there. I'll watch him until he goes to them, even if it's not right away. This is the only way."

"I'm going with you," Stein said from the corner of the room. She stood up straighter.

"I'm her partner. I'll go." Diego put up his hand in protest.

Erica took a step closer, wanting Diego to hear her words as a friend, not just a cop. "You can't go. It took everything you had not to shoot him at his house. If you lose your head, this whole thing could blow up."

He listened and then glanced over at Stein. "Is your gun qualification up-to-date?"

Stein patted her hip. "I'm a cop, Rodriguez. Just because I do the crime lab work here too, doesn't change that. I can do this, and she needs backup."

The chief pulled the door open. "If they aren't there, or if this isn't our guy, this could be a lawsuit for the department. I'll have to take disciplinary action." The door shut behind him. Erica didn't miss the fact he hadn't said *not* to do it.

"I'll drop him off at his place in forty-five minutes. If I haven't heard from you after thirty minutes, I'm coming back to the property to find you. No exceptions." Diego hugged her. He was warm and strong, and he smelled of the aftershave his wife bought him every year for his birthday. Then he looked over at Stein. "Don't do anything stupid and don't get killed."

She nodded, a bit surprised those were his only instructions. "Good plan."

For the first time since Erica had figured out Lucy was missing, she felt a small sense of relief. They had a plan, and she would stop at nothing to get Lucy and Jessica back. She wouldn't let her mind wander to the possibilities of what could be happening to either of them. She needed to focus on getting them out as soon as possible. It didn't matter what her chief had said about Frank Wilds not being their guy. She knew he was; she could feel it in every nerve ending of her body. He started this, but she was going to end it.

Chapter Thirty-one

Frank knew the room was purposely kept cold in an attempt to keep whoever was forced to sit in it uncomfortable. Despite this fact, he wasn't chilled. He looked down at the pictures in front of him, a beautiful display of his hard work for him to remember. These small-town cops were so far off the mark, he almost felt embarrassed for them.

That bitch cop Erica Chance would probably overrule the only one who seemed to have the slightest bit of wit about him. *As if my idiot cousin could have pulled off something of this magnitude.* But they would all know soon enough, and they wouldn't be able to deny his brilliance. Lucy was going to make him immortal. She was going to make sure he was remembered the way he wanted to be, and no one would be able to take that from him. No one would tarnish his accomplishments. And then he would get rid of her. His hands warmed with the thought of taking Lucy's life away, to watch the spirit drain from her eyes. It would be perfect. Then he would take Jessica and they could disappear together.

He'd chosen not to ask for a lawyer when they arrested him because he knew damn well they didn't have a shred of evidence on him. It was only a matter of time before he'd be out of here and back with Jessica. If he'd asked for a lawyer, it would've implied he had something to hide, and he didn't. He'd been right in front of them the whole time and they did nothing. The dumb cops chased their tails, sniffing around, looking for scraps of evidence that never existed. He was no amateur. He had been doing this for decades and across several different states. These small-town cops didn't have a chance in hell of figuring any of this out.

Diego walked in, heat and anger bubbling right at the surface. He knew the look well, because he felt it too. He thought about how ironic it was that they shared this commonality. The only thing that separated them was the fact that he had enough balls to act on it. This cop was restrained by the constructs of society, feeling as if he had to live a particular way to be accepted. That very idea went against the most very basic of human instincts. Diego Rodriguez was weak and pathetic. *Unlike me.*

"What the fuck are you smiling about?"

Frank made sure to smile wider. "You."

"What about me?"

"You and I, we aren't all that different."

Diego leaned across the table, getting in his face. "I'm nothing like you."

"No? You don't feel hatred pumping through your veins right now, every nerve ending in your body screaming at you to rip my head off?"

"You have something to confess, Wilds?"

He leaned closer to Diego, so close he could see the growing stubble on his cheek. "No, just making a point. We all have forces that drive us, forces beyond our own sense of reason. It's animalistic, that fury you're feeling right now. You should embrace it, be a man."

He watched as Diego's fists clenched on the table. "Get up. I'm taking you home."

Frank stood, feeling empowered, victorious. "Where's the woman?"

"Breakfast."

He shoved him out the door and down the hallway toward the parking lot in the back of the building. "Can I expect this harassment to continue, Detective?"

"No. We have nothing to hold you on." He took a deep breath. "We're releasing you, along with an apology."

Look at that, I even get an apology. It was poetic really, the police department driving him back to his house. Back to where he kept the very things they sought out so tirelessly. A part of him felt sorry for them. They were tied up, restrained by society's rules and expectations. They would never know freedom the way he did. The ability to take a human life, to make a decision religious institutions taught only God could make. *This will be it.* They would leave him alone now. He would have an endless amount of time with Jessica. And Lucy, well, she would be there to document it all.

❖

Erica and Stein worked their way along the fence line outside of his property until they were directly behind the barn. There were a few missing slats along the back of the structure, making it possible to see in. It wasn't perfect, but it was all they had. From this angle, they'd be able to see his movements inside the barn while still under the cover of the trees and dying shrubs.

Stein slipped her handgun into its holster as she knelt down next to her. "They've got to be in there."

Erica wiped the sweat off her forehead but didn't put away her gun. "I know, but we can't risk blowing this on a technicality." She looked down at her watch. "He'll be here soon."

Stein pulled a few of the branches back, then took out a small set of binoculars from her pocket and adjusted the sight. "I hope you're right about this."

"I am." She looked over at her, briefly breaking her focus from the barn. "Thanks for coming, by the way. You didn't have to do that."

"Don't get all sentimental," she whispered. "I would have done it for any cop."

"I know, but you did it for me and I wanted to thank you."

"You're not getting soft on me are you, Chance?"

"Nope."

"Can I ask you something?"

"Sure."

"Would we be here if we were just coming for Jessica, or are we here because of Lucy?"

Erica considered this question for a moment. Lucy was in danger, she could feel it, and she knew somewhere deep down in a place she couldn't identify, that this man had her. The very thought of it made her blood pump with a fury she had never experienced. But was Lucy more important than Jessica? No, there were people in this world that needed Jessica to exist, the same way she needed Lucy to exist. "I'd be here either way."

Stein watched her face, probably trying to decide if she was telling the truth. "Good, I would hate to be caught up in some insane romantic gesture."

"Shh. I hear a car."

They waited for what seemed like ages. The smell of dirt and foliage tickled her nose. Erica looked down at her watch for the ninth or tenth time. All she could assume was that Frank was waiting to make sure Diego was truly gone before coming into the barn. And he would, especially with his renewed confidence that the police were on the wrong track. He would be here soon. *Unless we're wrong, and it's not the barn he's using after all.* Ten acres was a lot of land, but she couldn't imagine him keeping them far from his house. He'd want control, and that meant having them nearby and isolated.

Just when she was beginning to formulate a new plan, they heard the sound of boots kicking through dirt, moving closer to them. Erica and Stein watched him move through the barn and over to the corner, where he pulled a tarp off a table and then slid it out of the way. Then he pulled open a large metal door and headed down a flight of stairs and out of sight.

She squeezed her fingers tighter around her gun. *I was right, you son of a bitch.* She felt the thrum of adrenaline start to pump through her body. They were minutes and feet away from putting an end to this nightmare. She wanted to get closer. She needed to hear what was going on down there without putting Jessica or Lucy in danger. Knowing Diego, he wasn't far away, and when she didn't check in, he'd be there in an instant as backup. Sweat slid down her back and arms, cooling her heated body. She felt sharp, focused, and determined. *This ends now.*

CHAPTER THIRTY-TWO

Lucy heard the door open and was surprised by the amount of light that poured into the makeshift dungeon. Her eyes had adjusted hours ago, and she was forced to squint at their captor.

"Sorry it took me so long to get back down here. I got held up." He moved toward Jessica. "Are you enjoying your present?"

She nodded, moving closer to Lucy.

Lucy stepped farther in front of her. "Why don't you let her go and I'll stay with you. I'll write your story and then I'll go with you, wherever you want. You don't need her. I'm the one who can preserve your legacy."

He laughed, a fully belly laugh, the kind that takes over your whole body and brings tears to your eyes. "Why would I ever want to do that? Look at her, she's perfect." He reached to touch her, and Jessica moved farther behind Lucy.

"No one is going anywhere."

The statement came from Erica. Lucy would have recognized the voice anywhere. It was strong and determined. It was exactly what Lucy had been begging whatever gods existed to hear.

Frank's face momentarily froze. Then, within a heartbeat, he was behind Lucy, a gun against her temple. The steel was cold against her face and the pressure instantly made her head throb.

Stein came down the stairs after Erica, gun already drawn and pointed in their direction. She stood next to Erica, trained on the same target. "Jessica, come over here. It's time to go."

Lucy looked over at Jessica. Her eyes were filled with panic, and she looked frozen to the spot. "Go. You have to go."

Frank pushed the gun harder into her temple. Her ears were buzzing and her head was swimming. She was terrified and relieved at the same time. Her instincts were telling her to run, but she willed her body to stay in place, not wanting to make the wrong move and put everyone in more danger.

He looked at Jessica. "If you go with them, I'll kill her."

Erica took a step forward. "And then I'll kill you."

He laughed, gripping Lucy's arm harder and shoving her forward. "But can you get me before I get them both, Detective? I don't think you can, and I don't think you'll risk it."

"You're out of your league, Wilds. There are going to be police all over the place in about five minutes. You have nowhere to go."

He bounced on the balls of his feet, shaking Lucy as he did it. "Let them come. It will be too late!" He said it with such force, spit sprayed from his mouth.

Stein moved to her right, putting distance between her and Erica, getting closer to Lucy. Her movements were fluid and practiced. "I have a shot."

Frank turned in her direction, forcing Lucy's body around with him. "Don't you feel foolish? If you had been any smarter, you could have prevented their deaths. They all cried out for someone to save them, but you were too late."

"You aren't going to hurt anyone ever again, Wilds."

Frank took three steps back, dragging Lucy with him. Lucy could feel her heart in her throat. Her brain was rapidly trying to assess the situation, attempting to play out each scenario. But did people get to cheat death twice? Was she going to get another chance? She watched Erica's sharp eyes, but they weren't focused on Wilds, they were focused on her.

There's so much I haven't said. So much she needs to know. "I'm sorry I got mad and got out of the car. I'm sorry I didn't call when your grandpa died. I'm sorry I stayed away for so long."

Frank pulled her closer. "Shut the fuck up."

But she wasn't going to shut up. She had stayed quiet for too long, and now, with death pressing against her head, she couldn't leave anything unsaid. "But mostly, I'm sorry for not spending every day of the last twelve years telling you just how much I love you. Because I do, and I always have. You always have been, and still are, the only one for me, Chance."

Frank pulled her head backward and put his mouth against her so she could feel the wetness of his mouth, his spit on the inside of her ear. "I told you to shut the fuck up."

His need to control the situation, his need to exude his power, was his downfall. While he was focused on Lucy, Erica darted along the other side of him. Now, with Stein on one side and Erica on the other, he looked back and forth frantically.

"It's over, Frank," Stein said from the right.

"It's over when I say it's over." He pointed his gun in Stein's direction and a loud blast came from the left.

The blast shook the small space that had suddenly become the size of a closet. Lucy couldn't hear anything, the sound of the gunshot filling her ears. She jerked forward out of his grip and stumbled to Jessica, who fell against her, sobbing. Frank fell to his knees and a large red star grew on his right shoulder. He lifted his right hand again, but Erica was already on top of him. She kicked the gun away and shoved him to the ground. She put her knee in the middle of his back and put handcuffs on him. She had wanted to kill him. She had wanted to enact retribution on him for everything he had done and had wanted to do. But he had used Lucy as cover and she couldn't get the clear kill shot without putting her in danger. It wasn't a risk she was willing to take.

Frank struggled underneath her. "You two bitches are going to wish you killed me. This isn't over."

Stein rushed over to Jessica, helping her to her feet. Lucy backed away, still off kilter from the gunshot and her declaration to Erica. She felt dizzy, and she could smell the desert heat and metallic scent of bombs and bullets. She was about ready to slump to the ground when she felt a hand on her back. It had to be Erica's hand. She turned into her, allowing her stress and fear to pour out of her in the form of tears against her shoulder. She wasn't sure how Erica felt about what she had said, but she didn't care. She needed Erica to hold her.

The police were there within minutes, and as they descended the stairs, her brother practically tackled her, pulling her away from Erica's embrace.

"Thank God you're okay." His arms were like vice grips around her body. She hugged him back, appreciating his presence but wanting to be back with Erica. "You need to be checked out by the paramedics."

Lucy automatically answered. "I'm fine."

He put his arm around her, walking her toward the stairs. "Humor me so I can tell Mom you got medical attention."

The sunshine was a renewing force on her face, warming away the cold, damp space she'd been held in. She sat next to Jessica in the back of an ambulance. EMTs were swarming all around them. There were lights in her eyes, a blood pressure band around her arm. She was aware of them around her, but she couldn't take her eyes off Erica. She needed to talk to her; she needed to be near her. She was about to push all of the EMTs out of the way and go to her when Jessica held her hand.

Lucy looked at the hand on top of hers. Fingernails covered in dirt that Jessica would probably spend the next several months scrubbing, thinking that remnants were still there, even if she couldn't see them.

"Thank you for everything, Lucy."

"I'll give you my number, if you ever need to talk."

"I take it that's your Zack?" She looked over at Erica.

"Yeah, that's my Zack."

Jessica smiled and was about to say something else when two sets of arms wrapped around her. Lucy could only assume they were her parents by the way they cried, overjoyed with happiness.

Lucy backed away from the family only to be trampled by her own. The sensation was overwhelming. Her parents, whom she assumed didn't realize anything had happened until several hours ago, were showering her with kisses and tears.

Her mom grabbed her face, kissing her again. "I'm never letting you out of my sight, ever again."

"I'm okay, Mom." She wanted to reassure her mom that she was okay, but she was enjoying the closeness all the same. She hadn't realized how badly she needed the familiar comfort until now.

❖

Erica stood off to the side of the car, watching Frank Wilds be shoved into the backseat. Stein stood next to her, arms crossed, smiling. He was trying to yell something from the backseat, and Stein put her hand up to her ear, pointing like she couldn't hear him. She even gave a little wave as the car pulled away.

The chief walked over and put a hand on her shoulder. "Nice work, you two."

"Thanks, Chief," they said in unison.

Erica looked over at Lucy, who was being smothered by her family.

Stein bumped her. "That was quite the confession down there."

Erica nodded, knowing she was talking about Lucy, not Wilds. "Yeah."

"You don't sound too excited. I kind of figured that was exactly what you had wanted to hear."

Erica continued to watch Lucy talk to her family. "I've waited years to hear everything she said down there. I think I'm just now starting to process it. There were a lot of things happening all at once."

Stein grinned. "And you always talk about what a great multitasker you are." She rolled her eyes. "So, what are you going to do about it now?"

Erica took a deep breath, still trying to take in the gravity of how quickly her life had just changed. "I'm going to talk to her about it."

"Well, that's boring. I was hoping for something a bit saucier."

"I live to keep you on your toes."

Stein chuckled and started toward the police cruiser. "Let's get all this crappy paperwork out of the way so you can go get your girl."

Diego approached her, a smile stretching from ear to ear. "We're going to take her home. Come over for a BBQ?"

Erica answered without thinking. "Sounds good."

She watched as he quickly made his way back over to his family. She wanted to follow him. She wanted to pull Lucy aside and talk to her then and there. She wanted to tell her how she felt, and how she'd heard every word she said. But that would have to wait. Erica needed to wrap up the paperwork for this case, and she wanted to talk to Lucy alone. She wanted to hear her say the things she'd said once more, but this time without a gun to her head. She wanted to hold her without anyone waiting for attention. She wanted...time.

Chapter Thirty-three

Lucy dabbed her temple with a bag of peas her mother had given her. She pulled the towel tighter around her body and stared in the mirror. There were no visible marks this time, no scars, no blood, but the emotional ones would remain long after today.

Grayson came in and flopped down on the bed, Holly right behind. "I want to ask you like a million questions, but Diego said not to push you. So I'm just going to sit here patiently until you're ready to talk to me."

"You may be waiting a while."

"Seriously, if you need to talk, I'm here."

Lucy didn't want to talk, not about what had happened, not about how she felt. She sat on the bed and ran her hand over Holly's face. "I think we need to head home tomorrow."

"What?" He sat up immediately.

"I have a major story to write, maybe the second biggest one of my life. I need to get back to work. I need normal." Her declaration to Erica had opened her up like a soda, and emotions she'd long held at bay were constantly flooding her. Memories of her time in war zones spread through her like poison ivy, but she couldn't scratch the mental images that flashed in front of her, or block the smell of cordite and blood. It was all too overwhelming, so she turned to her work, the only outlet that served to focus and ground her.

"What about Erica?"

What about Erica? That was a great question. She had poured her heart out to her, in front of everyone, and then Erica had gone on with her work like nothing had happened. Sure, it might have been a moment where she didn't know if her life was going to end, but it had been the truth all the same. Erica had been too busy with the case to talk to her. She was left vulnerable and raw. And more than that, she was hopeful. She needed to talk to Erica, to find out if their feelings were mutual.

"I'm going to talk to her, but that doesn't change the fact that I need to work too." She leaned down and kissed Holly's nose.

"Okay, if you want to go back, we'll go back."

Lucy walked back over to the mirror, letting her hair fall out of the towel. "You make it sound like you're doing me a favor. Were you going to stay in Clearbrook?"

"No, but I might be making a trip out to New York soon."

She started brushing her hair. "For what?"

He walked up behind her, gently pushed her into a chair, and continued brushing. "To see MJ."

"MJ? My brother?" She was confused, and it wasn't because of the bump on her head.

"Do you know another?"

"I just don't understand why." She was suddenly even more exhausted than she had been moments before.

"We like each other," he said plainly.

"You what?" She turned around in her chair.

He turned her back around and kept working on her hair. "Your brother is bi."

"No, he's not." Her tone was more accusatory than she had intended, but she couldn't help it.

"Ew. Don't get all biphobic."

"I'm not. I just had no idea." She sighed, wondering what else she didn't know about her family.

"Well, he hasn't exactly told your family yet."

Lucy thought back to what Erica had said. *She knew.* "You sure about that?"

"Your parents don't know. And you aren't going to be the one to tell them."

"And you're going to date someone who's in the closet?" She was concerned about what this could do to Grayson.

"Not normally, but I really like him. I want to see where this goes."

"It's going nowhere. MJ is a womanizer, a player, and it's going to end badly. I have watched him go through woman after woman. He has a cycle, and you're about to become part of it." She probably should have worded her warning plea better, but she couldn't rein in all of her emotions.

He turned her around in her chair and knelt in front of her, putting his hands on her legs. "I know you're going through a lot right now. More than I can possibly ever hope to understand. For that reason, I'm going to say this as nicely as I possibly can. But don't project your bullshit on me. We like each other and we are going to see where it goes."

She wasn't trying to project anything; she just didn't want to see Grayson get hurt. MJ was always looking for the next best thing, always thinking the grass was greener on the other side. *Wasn't that exactly what I thought when I left Erica?* "Okay, you're right. Good luck."

He stood, pulling her hair back. "Don't say good luck like you're sending me off to a war zone. It's just New York. I hear they have good bagels out there, and you know I love a good bagel."

Erica paced her living room, Bella watching each pass, watching her. "I eat over there at least once a week. Tonight's no different and we finally caught him. We should be happy."

Bella yawned and Erica nodded. "I know, thank you for agreeing. Okay, so we'll just go over there and eat. No big deal.

I'll find Lucy and we'll talk. We'll finally get all of this out in the open. I'll tell her that I do still have feelings for her and that we should give it another try. Easy, right?"

Bella let her legs scoot out in front of her until her body lay flush against the floor, her ears falling beside her head, giving her a melting effect. "What? You don't agree? Of course you agree. You love Lucy." She sat down on the floor next to Bella and put a hand on her back. "We can do this, Bella. I mean, hell, I shot someone today. This is nothing." She touched her head. "Want to go see Grandpa and Grandma?" Bella pushed her body upright and ran to the table to grab her leash. She trotted back over a moment later with it in her mouth. "Okay, let's go."

A few minutes later, she pulled up alongside the familiar house and put the car in park. She had been to this house thousands of times in her life. It was like a second home. The tree out front still had *Lucy + Erica Forever* carved in the trunk. Erica had carved it two years before they had ever kissed, her soul knowing long before she did that Lucy was who it desired. They had sworn to be friends forever, no matter what happened.

Bella started whining when Miguel walked out the front door waving. Erica opened the car door, and Bella took off across the street, running to him. Erica picked up the leash and tossed it back into the car, wondering why she even bothered to bring it.

Miguel opened the door for Bella, who trotted in to be welcomed by Sofia and Maria, who showered her with hugs and kisses and what looked like a small hamburger.

Miguel surprised her by pulling her into a big hug. "Thank you, *mija*. Thank you."

Erica hugged him back, understanding how grateful he was for his daughter's safety. Little did he know how grateful she was, too. After a moment, he patted her back. "Let's go inside."

Three things were always true of the Rodriguez house—there was always too much food, there was always plenty of beer, and it was always much louder than you would have thought possible for the amount of people inside. Erica saw Lucy right away, sitting in a corner, holding her niece and in what looked like a serious conversation with her sister-in-law. Her heart sped up when she noticed how beautiful she was. She took in a deep breath, knowing she was making the right decision. But she didn't want to interrupt their conversation, so she headed outside to get a drink. She'd find the perfect time.

She walked into the backyard where Diego and MJ were throwing a football back and forth. She opened the cooler and took out a beer, watching the two men behave like they were fifteen all over again. Grayson sat off to the side on the bench, watching them play. He saw Erica and patted the seat next to him.

She sat and took a sip of beer. "Careful, you're in the hit zone over here. Diego doesn't have as accurate of an arm as he thinks." Not a moment later, a football came whizzing by and MJ trotted by to retrieve it. "Told you."

Grayson picked up his beer off the ground, now aware of the danger. "How are you? I would ask you for details, but I know you must be tired of reliving it."

"I'm okay."

"Eventful day."

She looked over at MJ who winked in their direction. "I see you've caught MJ's eye."

"Is he as dangerous as Lucy makes him sound?"

"No, he just hasn't found what he's looking for." She had always thought this of MJ. He had a huge heart; he just hadn't found the right person to invest it in.

"Oh, I like how you word things. So much better than Lucy."

"Yeah, well, Lucy has always been very black-and-white. She's never really been able to see the gray area, you know, the place most of us live."

"Oh, you don't have to tell me. I think it's a reporter thing."

"Maybe. But she's been that way since we were kids."

"Well, then it must have been her calling. I mean, she just went through a traumatic event and she doesn't even want to take any time off. We're headed back down to San Diego tomorrow."

The words were like a punch in the stomach. "You are?"

Grayson answered, but he was focused on MJ's every move. "Yeah, she says she needs to get back and write this story. I suggested writing it from here, but she wants to go back. I swear her very last days are going to be spent in front of a laptop somewhere, trying to scoop her last story."

Erica knew he was talking, she saw his mouth moving, but she didn't hear what he was saying. She knew what she needed to do, and she wasn't going to let the fear of the unknown or the possibility of something going wrong stop her. She wasn't going to lose Lucy again, not without telling her what she felt.

She walked into the house and found her sitting on the couch alone, looking tired and contemplative. When she saw Erica approaching, she sat up straighter. Erica couldn't read the expression on her face, but she looked guarded.

"Can I talk to you for a minute?" Her heart was hammering. She could feel it in every part of her body.

"Sure." She got up and led the way out the front door.

Erica pulled the door closed, buying herself a few extra seconds, trying to work out exactly what she wanted to say. She turned and looked at Lucy. Her arms were crossed and her shoulders were scrunched. She looked so vulnerable, so unlike her usual confident self. Erica had been scared to bare her soul. She wasn't now, and she wouldn't be anymore. She thought about what to say next, but there were no words that could articulate what she felt.

So instead, she took a step closer and framed Lucy's face with her hands. Lucy's eyes searched Erica's for an answer. Erica leaned down and kissed her. She summoned all the long nights apart, all the missed days, all of the love she had and that still remained for her. She kissed her until she felt Lucy's arms come around her neck, pulling her in. And then she kissed her a little longer.

"I still love you too." She pulled away from her mouth just far enough to breathe out the words.

Lucy put her hands on her waist and pulled her against her, even harder now. "I'm sorry."

Erica kissed her forehead. "No more of that. No more 'I'm sorrys.'"

"I've missed you so much." Lucy put her forehead against Erica's chest, and ran her hands up and down her back.

"We have some things to figure out." Erica kissed the top of her head.

"Like what?" Lucy's hands froze.

"Like how frequent flyer miles work."

Lucy kissed her again and allowed her hands to travel back up Erica's back. She could feel her smiling. And for the first time since the last time she kissed Lucy so many years ago, she knew everything was going to be okay.

CHAPTER THIRTY-FOUR

Seven Months Later

Lucy slid the last box into the U-Haul and stared up at her apartment building for what would be the last time. She never imagined she would be moving back to Clearbrook, but here she was, giddy with anticipation. She would be starting her new job with the *San Francisco Chronicle* in a week, and she was thrilled. She even received a signing bonus to come up there, and would actually be getting her own office. Everything had fallen into place, even better than she had hoped.

Grayson slid the door shut and put the lock on the back. "You couldn't think of anything more cliché than renting a U-Haul?"

Lucy patted the back of the truck. "I did this so that you could tease me the whole drive up."

"And I will." He chugged a bottle of water.

"We wouldn't expect anything less, Grayson." Erica walked up beside her, putting her arm around her waist.

They had spent almost every weekend together since Erica made the first trip, and Lucy's heart still caught in her throat when Erica touched her. She craved her touch, her smile, the way she would go on and on about political issues, even the way she would subconsciously chew on her knuckle when she read a book. The little girl Erica once was was still there, peeking her head out sometimes when they would chase each other around the kitchen for something Lucy had said. But this version was better than anything she could have imagined.

Erica had grown into a strong, beautiful, sweet, passionate adult. She was everything Lucy had always hoped to find in someone. Her only regret was spending so long pretending that it hadn't always been Erica. Their time together, getting to know each other again, playing, laughing, having mind-blowing sex... it was so precious, and she reveled in every moment. Wrapped in Erica's arms at night, she slept better than she had in years, and even her nightmares had mostly abated. When one still happened, Erica was there to soothe her and bring her back to the present.

The Frank Wilds case had turned out to be a major turning point for both their careers. When Lucy's story broke, Clearbrook PD was contacted by agencies from four different states. Erica and Diego met with all the agencies and gathered together a vast amount of information, which ultimately ended with Frank Wilds confessing to the murders. His confession meant they'd taken the death penalty off the table, and he'd been handed eight life sentences in San Quentin State Prison. Families of the women who had died at the hands of Frank Wilds were finally able to gain some closure, and hopefully, peace. He had been responsible for a total of eight murders over the course of his quarter-century killing spree. Now these communities and families finally had a face to attach to the monstrosities they lived through, not just a phantom. Lucy wasn't sure if that was a blessing or a curse, but knew from experience closure meant more than most people would ever understand.

Lucy still kept in touch with Jessica. She was doing her best to find some peace and normalcy after her painful and terrifying experience with Frank Wilds. Jessica had briefly toyed with the idea of taking a year off from college, but had ultimately decided against it. She did, however, change her major to psychology. She wanted to be able to help people that had been through traumatic events. Lucy was proud of her for turning her situation into something positive, for herself and her community. Zack had been the picture of understanding and had never left her side. Only three days ago, she and Erica had received an invitation to their wedding for the following fall.

Bella lay on the grass beside the truck, able to sleep anywhere at any time. Holly was curled up next to her, best friends already.

Grayson walked over, picked up Holly, and nuzzled her face. "Can she ride with me in this hideous truck thing? She hates your music."

Lucy smiled, knowing this was his way of saying how much he would miss the little ball of fluff. "Yeah, I'm sure she would really like that."

"When are you moving to New York?" Erica joked.

"Not anytime soon." He slid his sunglasses down his nose. "Have you seen the weather reports out there? It's like eight degrees there right now. I didn't even realize that was a thing. Why would I leave this?" He swung his arm around in a tight circle above his head. "Your brother's cute, but he ain't that cute."

"We'll see." Erica pointed at him.

Grayson slid his sunglasses back up on his face and tossed his head back, walking toward the driver's seat like he was getting into a limo.

Erica turned and looked at Lucy. She placed her hands on either side of her face and kissed her forehead. "You ready?"

Lucy looked up and kissed her. "I have been waiting for this chance my whole life."

Erica rolled her eyes. "I see what you did there." She walked toward the driver's side of the car.

Lucy opened the backseat and let Bella hop in. "This is my last chance."

"You're very clever."

"I'm so glad you took a chance on me." Lucy laughed.

"Have you been saving these up?"

Lucy leaned over and kissed her. "By chance are you busy for say, the next thirty years?"

"Okay, now you're really pushing it." But Erica turned into the kiss, pulling Lucy in and letting her mouth linger over her own.

"You love it." She reached across the seat and put her hand on top of Erica's, loving the way it felt when their fingers were intertwined.

Erica picked up their hands and kissed the top of Lucy's. "I do, and I love you."

Erica's phone rang, and she hit the talk button on the steering wheel. "Detective Chance."

"Detective, I hate to do this to you, but we're going to need you. I know you're on vacation, but we need you back up here ASAP."

"What's the problem, Chief?"

"I'll uh…I'll explain it when you get back up here, but it isn't pretty. Rodriguez is on it now, but we could use your help."

"I'll come in first thing in the morning. We're leaving San Diego now."

"Thanks, Chance, sorry about this." The phone line went dead.

Erica looked over at her. "Sorry. I'm going to have to go in as soon as we get back."

"I understand, and it's okay." Lucy meant what she said. She had been in the reporting field long enough to know that there are certain jobs that you don't get to clock in and clock out at the same time every day. Being a detective was one of those jobs, and Erica knew there might be assignments Lucy had to suddenly take off for as well. "Hey, this is what I signed up for. And maybe it will be a good story for me to cover."

"You going to change your mind?"

Lucy leaned over and kissed her cheek. "Never."

Erica smiled at her response and Lucy, for the millionth time, thanked whatever force was responsible for things like this in the world, for bringing Erica back to her. Erica always had been and always would be, Lucy's Chance.

About the Author

Jackie D was born and raised in the San Francisco, East Bay Area of California. She now resides in Central Pennsylvania with her wife and their numerous furry companions. She earned a bachelor's degree in recreation administration and a dual master's degree in management and public administration. She is a Navy veteran and served in Operation Iraqi Freedom as a flight deck director, onboard the USS Abraham Lincoln.

She spends her free time with her wife, friends, family, and their incredibly needy dogs. She enjoys playing golf but is resigned to the fact she would equally enjoy any sport where drinking beer is encouraged during game play. Her first book, Infiltration, was a finalist for a Lambda Literary Award.

Books Available from Bold Strokes Books

Change in Time by Robyn Nyx. Working in the past is hell on your future. The Extractor series: Book Two (978-1-62639-880-1)

Love After Hours by Radclyffe. When Gina Antonelli agrees to renovate Carrie Longmire's new house, she doesn't welcome Carrie's overtures at friendship or her own unexpected attraction. A Rivers Community Novel. (978-1-63555-090-0)

Nantucket Rose by CF Frizzell. Maggie Jordan can't wait to convert an historic Nantucket home into a B&B, but doesn't expect to fall for mariner Ellis Chilton, who has more claim to the house than Maggie realizes. (978-1-63555-056-6)

Picture Perfect by Lisa Moreau. Falling in love wasn't supposed to be part of the stakes for Olive and Gabby, rival photographers in the competition of a lifetime. (978-1-62639-975-4)

Set the Stage by Karis Walsh. Actress Emilie Danvers takes the stage again in Ashland, Oregon, little realizing that landscaper Arden Philips is about to offer her a very personal romantic lead role. (978-1-63555-087-0)

Strike a Match by Fiona Riley. When their attempts at matchmaking fizzle out, firefighter Sasha and reluctant millionairess Abby find themselves turning to each other to strike a perfect match. (978-1-62639-999-0)

The Price of Cash by Ashley Bartlett. Cash Braddock is doing her best to keep her business afloat, stay out of jail, and avoid Detective Kallen. It's not working. (978-1-62639-708-8)

Under Her Wing by Ronica Black. At Angel's Wings Rescue, dogs are usually the ones saved, but when quiet Kassandra Haden meets outspoken owner Jayden Beaumont, the two stubborn women just might end up saving each other. (978-1-63555-077-1)

Underwater Vibes by Mickey Brent. When Hélène, a translator in Brussels, Belgium, meets Sylvie, a young Greek photographer and swim coach, unsettling feelings hijack Hélène's mind and body—even her poems. (978-1-63555-002-3)

A More Perfect Union by Carsen Taite. Major Zoey Granger and DC fixer Rook Daniels risk their reputations for a chance at true love while dealing with a scandal that threatens to rock the military. (978-1-62639-754-5)

Arrival by Gun Brooke. The spaceship *Pathfinder* reaches its passengers' new homeworld where danger lurks in the shadows while Pamas Seclan disembarks and finds unexpected love in young science genius Darmiya Do Voy. (978-1-62639-859-7)

Captain's Choice by VK Powell. Architect Kerstin Anthony's life is going to plan until Bennett Carlyle, the first girl she ever kissed, is assigned to her latest and most important project, a police district substation. (978-1-62639-997-6)

Falling Into Her by Erin Zak. Pam Phillips, widow at the age of forty, meets Kathryn Hawthorne, local Chicago celebrity, and it changes her life forever—in ways she hadn't even considered possible. (978-1-63555-092-4)

Hookin' Up by MJ Williamz. Will Leah get what she needs from casual hookups or will she see the love she desires right in front of her? (978-1-63555-051-1)

King of Thieves by Shea Godfrey. When art thief Casey Marinos meets bounty hunter Finnegan Starkweather, the crimes of the past just might set the stage for a payoff worth more than she ever dreamed possible. (978-1-63555-007-8)

Lucy's Chance by Jackie D. As a serial killer haunts the streets, Lucy tries to stitch up old wounds with her first love in the wake of a small town's rapid descent into chaos. (978-1-63555-027-6)

Right Here, Right Now by Georgia Beers. When Alicia Wright moves into the office next door to Lacey Chamberlain's accounting firm, Lacey is about to find out that sometimes the last person you want is exactly the person you need. (978-1-63555-154-9)

Strictly Need to Know by MB Austin. Covert operator Maji Rios will do whatever she must to complete her mission, but saving a gorgeous stranger from Russian mobsters was not in her plans. (978-1-63555-114-3)

Tailor-Made by Yolanda Wallace. Tailor Grace Henderson doesn't date clients, but when she meets gender-bending model Dakota Lane, she's tempted to throw all the rules out the window. (978-1-63555-081-8)

Time Will Tell by M. Ullrich. With the ability to time travel, Eva Caldwell will have to decide between having it all and erasing it all. (978-1-63555-088-7)

A Date to Die by Anne Laughlin. Someone is killing people close to Detective Kay Adler, who must look to her own troubled past for a suspect. There she finds more than one person seeking revenge against her. (978-1-63555-023-8)

Captured Soul by Laydin Michaels. Can Kadence Munroe save the woman she loves from a twisted killer, or will she lose her to a collector of souls? (978-1-62639-915-0)

Dawn's New Day by TJ Thomas. Can Dawn Oliver and Cam Cooper, two women who have loved and lost, open their hearts to love again? (978-1-63555-072-6)

Definite Possibility by Maggie Cummings. Sam Miller is just out for good times, but Lucy Weston makes her realize happily ever after is a definite possibility. (978-1-62639-909-9)

Eyes Like Those by Melissa Brayden. Isabel Chase and Taylor Andrews struggle between love and ambition from the writers' room on one of Hollywood's hottest TV shows. (978-1-63555-012-2)

Heart's Orders by Jaycie Morrison. Helen Tucker and Tee Owens escape hardscrabble lives to careers in the Women's Army Corps, but more than their hearts are at risk as friendship blossoms into love. (978-1-63555-073-3)

Hiding Out by Kay Bigelow. Treat Dandridge is unaware that her life is in danger from the murderer who is hunting the woman she's falling in love with, Mickey Heiden. (978-1-62639-983-9)

Omnipotence Enough by Sophia Kell Hagin. Can the tiny tool that abducted war veteran Jamie Gwynmorgan accidentally acquires help her escape an unknown enemy to reclaim her stolen life and the woman she deeply loves? (978-1-63555-037-5)

Summer's Cove by Aurora Rey. Emerson Lange moved to Provincetown to live in the moment, but when she meets Darcy Belo and her son Liam, her quest for summer romance becomes a family affair. (978-1-62639-971-6)

The Road to Wings by Julie Tizard. Lieutenant Casey Tompkins, Air Force student pilot, has to fly with the toughest instructor, Captain Kathryn "Hard Ass" Hardesty, fly a supersonic jet, and deal with a growing forbidden attraction. (978-1-62639-988-4)

Beauty and the Boss by Ali Vali. Ellis Renois is at the top of the fashion world, but she never expects her summer assistant Charlotte Hamner to tear her heart and her business apart like sharp scissors through cheap material. (978-1-62639-919-8)

Fury's Choice by Brey Willows. When gods walk amongst humans, can two women find a balance between love and faith? (978-1-62639-869-6)

Lessons in Desire by MJ Williamz. Can a summer love stand a four-month hiatus and still burn hot? (978-1-63555-019-1)

Lightning Chasers by Cass Sellars. For Sydney and Parker, being a couple was never what they had planned. Now they have to fight corruption, murder, and enemies hiding in plain sight just to hold on to each other. Lightning Series, Book Two. (978-1-62639-965-5)

Summer Fling by Jean Copeland. Still jaded from a breakup years earlier, Kate struggles to trust falling in love again when a summer fling with sexy young singer Jordan rocks her off her feet. (978-1-62639-981-5)

Take Me There by Julie Cannon. Adrienne and Sloan know it would be career suicide to mix business with pleasure, however tempting it is. But what's the harm? They're both consenting adults. Who would know? (978-1-62639-917-4)

The Girl Who Wasn't Dead by Samantha Boyette. A year ago, someone tried to kill Jenny Lewis. Tonight she's ready to find out who it was. (978-1-62639-950-1)

Unchained Memories by Dena Blake. Can a woman give herself completely when she's left a piece of herself behind? (978-1-62639-993-8)

Walking Through Shadows by Sheri Lewis Wohl. All Molly wanted to do was go backpacking…in her own century. (978-1-62639-968-6)

A Lamentation of Swans by Valerie Bronwen. Ariel Montgomery returns to Sea Oats to try to save her broken marriage but soon finds herself also fighting to save her own life and catch a murderer. (978-1-62639-828-3)

Freedom to Love by Ronica Black. What happens when the woman who spent her lifetime worrying about caring for her family, finally finds the freedom to love without borders? (978-1-63555-001-6)

House of Fate by Barbara Ann Wright. Two women must throw off the lives they've known as a guardian and an assassin and save two rival houses before their secrets tear the galaxy apart. (978-1-62639-780-4)

Planning for Love by Erin Dutton. Could true love be the one thing that wedding coordinator Faith McKenna didn't plan for? (978-1-62639-954-9)

Sidebar by Carsen Taite. Judge Camille Avery and her clerk, attorney West Fallon, agree on little except their mutual attraction, but can their relationship and their careers survive a headline-grabbing case? (978-1-62639-752-1)

Sweet Boy and Wild One by T. L. Hayes. When Rachel Cole meets soulful singer Bobby Layton at an open mic, she is immediately in thrall. What she soon discovers will rock her world in ways she never imagined. (978-1-62639-963-1)

To Be Determined by Mardi Alexander and Laurie Eichler. Charlie Dickerson escapes her life in the US to rescue Australian wildlife with Pip Atkins, but can they save each other? (978-1-62639-946-4)

True Colors by Yolanda Wallace. Blogger Robby Rawlins plans to use First Daughter Taylor Crenshaw to get ahead, but she never planned on falling in love with her in the process. (978-1-62639-927-3)

Unexpected by Jenny Frame. When Dale McGuire falls for Rebecca Harper, the mother of the son she never knew she had, will Rebecca's troubled past stop them from making the family they both truly crave? (978-1-62639-942-6)